Precious

Cecile Tomb

Contents

Chapter 1

Caroline waited quietly outside her mistress bedroom. She nervously rolled her eyes as she heard moaning coming from the other side, "Yes.. Yes.."

As the door opened, Caroline stood and curtsied as an unknown gentleman left Lady Elizabeth's bed chamber. He paused at the young silent beauty, "Hmmm.. Perhaps next time?"

Caroline looked away as he walked past her. She sighed and entered her lady's room. She rolled her eyes at the naked woman that was passed out in bed. Tomorrow they would be leaving on their voyage for Lady Elizabeth to be wed. Caroline continued to pick up the discarded clothes and tucked Lady Elizabeth's bedding in around her. As she was about to leave she heard her mistress speak, "Thank you Caroline."

Caroline smiled a gentle smile and took her leave.

*******************Two weeks later

Lady Elizabeth sat in her cabin with heavy sea sickness. She would moan every time the boat would hit a massive wave. Caroline felt bad for her, "Liz, may I go and fetch you some fresh water to drink?"

Elizabeth pressed her eyes closed and nodded. Caroline made he way up to the deck so she could get some fresh air on the way to the galley. She breathed in the heavy night air. There was a thick fog on the water, Caroline walked slower as she looked to the the west side of the ship. She gasped and dropped the bucket as a dark ship eased out of the thick fog. Caroline counted the cannon doors to herself, "Fifteen.. Fifteen on this side, means thirty all together!" She took off in a sprint to reach her destination. Elizabeth shot up in her bed as Caroline busted in, "We are about to be boarded!"

Elizabeth wrinkled her brow as she shook her head.

Caroline swallowed loudly, "Pirates."

Elizabeth's lip quivered as she tried to stay calm, "Okay.. What do we do?"

Caroline was at a loss, she could only think of Elizabeth's safety. She was the most valuable cargo on this ship, "Give me your dress.."

Elizabeth cocked a questionable brow to her, "What?"

Caroline pulled her closer to her face, "Trust me.."

Byron smirked as he men silently overwhelmed the crew, "Too easy.."

His feet thundered on the wooden planks as he walked on board. His first mate approached him with a smile, "Sir, we have located her."

"Excellent, lead the way." Byron spread his devilish smile across his face as he entered the lavish cabin, "Good evening ladies."

Caroline and Elizabeth hugged each other as the man took a step closer, "Which one of you is Lady Elizabeth?"

The women did not speak.

Byron tilted his head as he looked them over, "That one. She's fairer of the two and the dress is finer."

Elizabeth's lip quivered as she realized the plan had worked. She tried to hang on to Caroline, but the man was too strong. She screamed, "No! No! No!"

One of Byron's men stepped forward as though he was about to attack but was stopped by Byron's arm, "Leave her."

Caroline hung her head as the man escorted her away from her loving friend. She had silent tears easing down her cheeks as Byron grabbed her by the waist and swung across to his ship. She gasped as she was shoved to a different seaman, "Take her to my chamber."

Caroline furiously shook her head as she stepped away, "No, please!"

The seaman pressed his teeth and slapped her, knocking her to the ground, "Get up wench!"

Caroline gasped at the man while he heaved as a sword was thrusted through him from behind.

The man fell to the side making Byron appear as the murder, "No need to damage the merchandise."

Caroline shook her freighted face as she tried to crawl away backwards.

Byron eased down and hoisted her over his shoulder as though she was light as a feather.

She was shocked as the men dumped the dead man's body over the side of the ship, then carried on as though nothing happened. Caroline pressed her eyes closed as the thought, "What is to become of me?"

Byron slung the young beauty on his bed and pinned her down. Carolines chest heaved as she felt the heat of his body, "I don't understand. Why would the Duke throw something away like you?"

Caroline wrinkled her brow, "What do you speak of?"

He smirked at his prisoner, "Your fiancé hired me to kidnap you. Said your looseness was an embarrassment."

Caroline grinned an evil smile with pressed teeth, "Well.. I suppose both of you lose. I'm not Elizabeth."

Byron's smile slowly disappeared, "What?"

She continued her mocking, "I switched places to protect her."

He growled, "You lie! And for lying you will be punished."

Caroline gulped at his freighting handsome features.

Chapter 2

"You make me sick."

Caroline scowled at her captor, "Me?! I've done nothing wrong!"

Byron chuckled as he poured himself a brandy, "Please.. Lady Elizabeth, you must be mistaken. Why would a servant risk their neck for the likes of you?"

She pushed herself off of the bed and stomped to him, "Because she was not only my mistress. She .. she..was..my.."

Byron pouted his lip, "Friend?"

Caroline couldn't believe this man's cruelty as tears eased down her cheeks. She whispered, "Yes.."

He scoffed, "The only friends that the wealthy care about, are their pockets."

"What were you planning on, once you had captured her?"

Byron was slowly losing his temper, "You mean you?"Caroline bravely searched his face. He rolled his eyes, "I'm going to sell you, if you really wanted to know."

Caroline held her abdomen as she stepped away, "Why would the Duke wish that upon her?"

He growled as he slammed down his glass, "That's enough!" He quickly spun around to the shaking girl, "You are Elizabeth! Now confess it!Before I have my first mate string you up naked and whipped before the entire crew!"

Caroline sobbed as he pressed her against the cabin wall, "I cannot confess sir. I am Caroline. I am her servant."

Byron stepped back away in disbelief, "No.. No!"

She eased her fear stricken eyes open, "Please, do not hate me for saving a friends life."

He turned away as he rubbed his face. He quietly thought to himself, "He had strict instructions, take Lady Elizabeth, but leave her maid. Why did he want Elizabeth out of the picture?" He placed his hands on both of his hips and looked up, "Quit crying!"

Caroline shook as she covered her mouth.

Byron slowly strutted to her, "So, if your really her maid; then you won't mind a little bit of hard work. Hmm?"

She lowered her hand and gasped as he dragged her to the pantry. Caroline huffed when he roughly sat her on a wooden chair, "You see all theses?" She shyly looked over the vast pile of potatoes and nodded. He smirked and tossed her a peel knife, "Get to work."

Carolines voice quivered, "How many sir?"

He smirked as he turned away, "Keep peeling until I come back."

She sighed loudly as she turned to the vast pile, shrugged and started her task.

*************Duke William Rochester smiled as The Victoria eased into port. He was immediately greeted by the captain as he boarded, "Sir William, we had a most unfortunate experience at sea.."

William smiled as he continued to walk to his fiancé cabin, "Oh really? What ever happened?"

"Well, Lady Elizabeth, her servant..."

William paused as he listened, "What of her?"

The captain gulped, "Another ship took her, only her, but your betrothed is safe sir."

"What?! William slammed the captain to the ships hall wall.

Elizabeth heard the commotion and investigated, "William, oh thank God!"

William immediately let go of his prisoner and embraced his future wife, "My dear, thank heavens you are alright."

Elizabeth started to sob, "William, they took her. They took Caroline. We must find them!"

William stroked Elizabeth's thick hair, "Ssshhh... We will find her." His eyes were in an evil stare, "I will make sure of it."

****

After being in the pantry for five hours, Byron stepped down into the dark room. He was amazed that over half of the potatoes were peeled. Sitting slumped over was a snoozing Caroline. He placed his hands on his hips and shook his head in amazement. He then eased the peeling blade from her hand and scooped her up bridal style. Once at his cabin he eased her down into the cabin boy hammock and briefly stood over her. She seemed very young, perfect figure, light brown thick hair that was in a long braid. He imagined once let down it would go past her bottom. Her neck was long and lean with a strong but short chin. Full pouty lips and perfect brow. After studying her features he was starting to realize she was extremely beautiful. Did the Duke also see her as this? There was more to this young woman than he knew, but planned on finding out.

Chapter 3

"Rise and shine!"

Caroline jumped at the booming voice, "What?.. What time is it?" She rubbed her sleepy eyes as she slightly pouted her perfect lip.

Byron chuckled as he thought she looked adorable, "An hour before sunrise. Now off to the mess hall with you."

Caroline tried to ease out of her hammock, but she lost her balance and fell with a thud to the floor. Her anger boiled as Byron stood over her and laughed. Unfortunately, her anger turned into helplessness, then tears. He leaned down to offer his hand, but she eased herself up without his assistants.

He pursed his lips at her stubbornness, "Its not polite to refuse a gentleman when he is trying to help."

She paused with a wrinkled brow, "Funny, I have yet to see any of those on board. When you find one, please point me in their direction, so I may have a little hope of my future."

Byron balled up his fist and stomped to her. Caroline took steps back and looked away as he pressed her against the wall, "Be very careful how you speak to me. I can be a humble host, or your worst nightmare. Is that clear?"

Caroline whimpered as she nodded. He liked being this close to her, but released her so she could be on her way.

After spending two hours in the kitchen, Caroline manned the food line for the crew. Byron and his first mate Sam stood back and watched from a distance, "Pretty is she not?"

Byron smile as he continued to watch her and nodded.

The men both found her sarcasm with the crew hilarious.

Caroline rolled her eyes as the fifth man made the same remark, "I would rather be eating you.."

"Yeah? So did the other fifteen.."

The next man that undressed her with his eyes, before he could speak she yelled, "Forget it! Next!" The man scowled at her and moved down the line.

The next one tried to touch her, she pursed her lips and smacked his hand with the metal ladle. The man jumped and shook his hand to ease the pain.

Byron and Sam had pressed eyes from their laughter.

Caroline growled at the sight of their amusement. She would love to poison Byron, but knew it would be her end, more ways than one.

As she glared at them, then the next voice in line was younger, "Miss? May I have a serving please?"

Caroline snapped out of her angered daze and to the young man's handsome face, "Oh, yes of course.." She blushed as she gave the polite man a smile.

He chuckled at her innocence, "Thank you ma'am."

She looked down, "Your welcome."

The young man didn't want to move but there were plenty of hungry sailors behind him waiting. Sam cut his eyes at the scene then back the a clenched jaw Byron, "Best you end that now captain?"

Byron didn't move his gaze from the young beauty, "Aye."

Before the young sailor took his seat, Byron put his muscular arm around him, "Pretty isn't she?"

The young man stuttered, "Yes sir.."

Byron eased an evil smile across his perfect teeth, "Just know, she is off limits. Is that clear?"

The young man nervously nodded, "Of course sir."

Byron paused for a moment and then patted his prisoner, "Good lad."

Caroline quickly looked away as Byron looked towards her. She felt bad for the young man, especially since he was the only one that had showed her any respect. If Byron found that intimidating, then obviously he was no gentleman.

As the last man was served, Caroline sighed and tried to scrape what little was left for her own meal. She slightly frowned since there was none left. ShePressed her eyes as she thought to herself, "You are not asking for food! You should not have to.. Right..?" Her eyes slowly eased open as she realized someone was standing in front of her. She looked up to Byron's face. He smirked and looked into the serving pot, "Hmm.. nothing left I see.."

Caroline stared past him, "No sir."

He was eager to hear her ask for something but knew better, "Hungry?"

She kept her stare locked as she controlled her temper, "Yes sir."

"Well.. May I please escort you to my chamber for our meal?"

She had to push the words out, "I would be delighted."

Byron laughed a low seductive laugh and offered her his arm. The crew watched as he turned to them, "Gentleman, a round of applause for our lovely server! This was her first and only appearance for your viewing pleasure!"

The crew stood and clapped as he escorted her away. Caroline was boiling mad, "Why did you do that?"

Byron laughed, "Caroline, they do not feel or see many women, let alone one as pretty you, so let's just say; I gave them all something to dream about."

Caroline closed her eyes in disgust, "They .. They.."

He bit his lip and nodded, "Oh yes, you guessed it."

She shivered then turned an angry brow to him as he closed the door.

Chapter 4

Caroline slowly savored her breakfast as Byron watched and stared, "Do you always eat so slow?"

Caroline slightly coughed as she swallowed her bite, "I beg your pardon?"

"You eat like a bird, but slowly, why?"

She slightly looked down then back to the handsome face sitting across from her, "I'm very tired sir. If I need to be finished..."

Byron rolled his eyes and held up his hand, "Tired? You haven't work a full day's work."

Caroline looked down as she tried to hold back angry tears, "What will be my next task sir?"

He was amused at her willingness to prove him wrong, "Do you know how to mend clothing?" She shyly nodded. "Excellent, I'll have Taylor bring the bundle in here."

Caroline didn't look up, "Yes sir."

Byron pondered why she was being so submissive, perhaps she was gladly taking these chores to earn her keep, instead of earning it in his bed. Of course he would prefer the other, but her type always annoyed him in the end. Lazy, needy and unfaithful. On the other hand, she was the prettiest woman he ever had that close for him to bed, free will or not. He watched her ease from her seat and started to clear the table. As she leaned in closed to him, he had the urge to pull her to his lap. Caroline could also feel an uneasy tension between them. With this she quickly stepped away to set the tray outside the door.

She continued to feel uneasy as he watched her every move, "Sir, why do you look at me so?"

Byron nibbled on the tip of his finger as he smirked, "Your nice to look at, haven't you been told before?"

She nervously looked away and shook her head, "No sir."

He cocked a questionable brow as he stepped towards her, "Hmm.. how else have men charmed you into their beds?"

Before she realized her actions, she gasped and slapped him across his face. She knew she would be punished, but her virtue was something she held dear.

Byron flexed his jaw from side to side, "Hmm.. touchy on the subject of you and your mistress past time?"

Caroline frowned with pain, "Why must you insult my virtues? I have done nothing to deserve this treatment."

Byron took another step closer, "You say your a servant, but I can clearly see you have lived a life of luxury. You are no better than them."

She turned her frowned gaze to the floor as she rubbed her scar that had been branded on the back of her neck. It seemed as though yesterday that it happened.

Byron studied her painful expression and actions, "What are you thinking?"

She didn't look up, "It "twas nothing."

He rolled his eyes and threw open his door to retreat to the deck of the ship. He couldn't get her painful expression from his mind. Maybe he was wrong to question her virtue, but he put his attention on his crew to feel less guilt.

After spending all day on deck, Byron gladly made his way into his chamber. Caroline was just finishing up on mending the last shirt of the large crew. He noticed how her plump lips slightly pouted as she focused on her task. Byron ached to pull her head up to kiss them, but snapped out the thought. His devilish grin spread across his mouth as he untucked his white shirt, "This one is next."

Caroline did a double take as her eyes widened, "Oh.. I.." She lost her train of thought at the sight of his sculpted chest. She cursed herself for blushing.

Byron tots the garment to her and laid in his bed as he watched her. She pouted her lip as she looked for the tear, "Sir, where is it ripped?"

He couldn't hide his amusement, "Oh, is there none?"

Caroline wrinkled her brow and threw it back to him. She shook her head as she proceeded to bundle up the garments and head to the laundry. She stopped when he spoke, "Go fetch hot water for my bath. She nodded and started to leave again, until he stepped her again, "I expect you to bath me."

She gulped loudly as she kept her gaze turned away.

Chapter 5

Caroline held her breath before she opened the cabin door. Her eyes gazed around the room. Her breath quivered as she noticed his shadow behind the dressing screen. She lightly walked with her pale of hot water and poured the last of the hot water into the iron tub. Her eyes frantically avoided the approaching footsteps as she poured. Caroline quickly turned away as a naked Byron eased into the water.

She jumped when she heard his voice, "Well.. What are you waiting for?"

She pressed her eyes closed as she heaved while rubbing her sweating hands on her apron. Caroline slowly turned to him and grabbed a cloth and soap. She eased down on her knees behind his head and stared to wet his hair with a tin cup.

Byron smirked as he moaned from the sensation. Caroline nervously looked away. She bit her lip when he spoke, "Now the rest of me."

Caroline eased from behind and leaned beside the tub and cleared her nervous throat while she scrubbed his muscular chest. She pressed her eyes again at his request, "Lower." Her hand shook as she scrubbed his hard stomach. Caroline could feel his eyes burning into her as he studied her.

He quietly thought to himself, "Why is she so nervous? She's beautiful, surly she's been with a man." He smirked as he tried to caress her cheek. She gasped as she pulled from his grasp. Caroline took slow steps backwards as Byron eased from the tub. She kept her large frightened eyes locked on his stern face.

He growled as he pinned her against the cabin wall, "What's the matter? Do you not find me handsome?"

Caroline shook as she turned her gaze away, "I didn't say that sir."

"Then why do you act like a little innocent school girl?" She muffled a small cry as he nuzzled his nose into her hair. He leaned back to her pain stricken face and then eased away back to the dressing screen. Caroline closed her eyes and sighed with relief.

After she cleared the tub, Byron made no attempt to give her privacy as she washed herself behind the dressing screen, using the wash basin. As much as he would like to see her in the tub fully naked, he knew her answer would be no. His devilish smile pressed across his handsome face as he could see little bits and pieces of soft flesh between the cracks of fabric and wood. He could feel his excitement growing the longer he watched. He snapped out of his lustful daze as reality kicked in, "She's for profit only. Don't even think about it." He rolled his eyes and focused on his charts.

As Caroline peaked from behind the screen, only his cold eyes cut to her, "What is it?"

She cleared her throat for encouragement, "Sir, if I may please sleep in my chemise, I would be ever so grateful."

He wrinkled his brow, "What is wrong with your dress?"

She bit her lip, "It's uncomfortable sir, but if you value your modesty, I.."

He cut her off with the raise of his hand, "Fine!"

Caroline sighed as she eased from behind the screen. His mouth went dry as he swallowed. Now he saw perfectly clear why she asked. His eyes kept them locked on her as she quickly tipped toed to her hammock. Byron wanted to badly scoop her up and throw her on his bed, but her little voice snapped him out of his daydream, "Goodnight."

He sighed a frustrating sigh, "Good night Caroline."

In the middle of the night, he towered over her as she slept. The moonlight from the window danced on her porcelain skin. Byron gently caressed her cheek, but did not disturb her.

As morning broke, Byron yawned and stretched. He jolted from the bed as he noticed his prisoner had escaped. He ran to the deck of the ship but froze as he saw her perfect form in the sunlight. By God she was beautiful. He growled as he noticed deck hands coming from under the ship we're watching her. Byron's anger boiled as he stepped to her. Her eyes shot open with as he grasped her arm, "What do you think you are doing?"

She gulped her fear down the best she could.

Chapter 6

Caroline whimpered as Byron roughly slung her into the cabin. She jumped as he slammed the door. Her chest heaved as she spun around to face him, "What! What have I done to offend you now?!"

He took heavy, slow steps to her shaking form, "What were you doing on deck?"

Carolines brow wrinkled with anger, "I only wished for some fresh air sir!"

Byron didn't touch her, but closely towered over her, "You stay in here at all times! Do you understand me?!"

She had a single tear streaked down her cheek, "May I please ask why?"

He continued to look down upon her shaking form, "For your protection of course." She raised a questionable brow to him, "You are worth more without a bastard in your belly."

Caroline felt discussed as his devilish grin spread across his lips, "Why do you hate me so?"

Byron sighed, "I don't hate you, I do hate your mistress on the other hand."

He turned to walk to his desk, "Why sir?"

He paused as he looked into a daze, "Her father destroyed someone dear to me. I will punish him through her, and I'll get to her with you."

Caroline looked down as she shook her head, "You seek revenge on a dead man. A man that placed his only child in a marriage agreement before his death. I swear to you, she is not like you think! Please, please believe me!"

Byron's expression eased as he turned to her, "Don't take it personal, this is only coincidental."

Caroline looked down as her lip quivered, "What cruelty was bestowed upon you? What has hardened your heart so it may bleed on to others?"

He was actually taken back buy her words, "I did not wish to become this. The world of the rich made me this monster."

Instead of hating him, Caroline actually felt pity for the handsome captor, "I understand."

Byron cocked an uneasy brow as he turned back to his charts. Caroline sighed and sat on a window seat, and stared over the vast ocean. After an hour of charting, Byron twisted his neck to pop it. He then cut his eyes over to a focused Caroline. She was in such deep thought with her drawing, she did not realize him looming over her.

"That looks nothing like the Saint Fury."

Caroline eased her calm surprised expression up to his scowl, "Well.. That's wonderful Capitan, since it is The Victoria. You remember, the ship you stole me from?"

Byron growled as he leaned away from her, "Is that all you have to do today?"

Caroline sighed as she continued her drawing, "What task do would you like me to do captain?"

He stood silently as he stroked his mouth, "I want you to draw my ship."

She slowly turned her eyes to him, "Sir, I would.."

"Yes, I know. You would have to be in port or another ship to see her from the side." He smirked as he stepped next to her, "You will get your chance, for we will be in Port Royal very shortly."

Caroline tried to hide her excitement as she wet her lips, "Why Port Royal sir?"

"I have business to discuss with an old friend and we need supplies."

Caroline looked back to her drawing as she thought of a plan of escape. She kept her gaze focused as he kneeled down beside her, "Don't even think about escaping. There are far worse ships and gentlemen than I."

She turned her sad eyes to him, their faces were very close to one another, "I understand." Her eyes cut down to Byron's full opened lips as he stared to lean in for a kiss. Caroline exhaled her breath as she turned her cheek to him and continued to draw. Byron growled as he shoved from the seat and out to the top deck. Caroline pressed her eyes as she thought, "I have to get away! I will get away! I have to find Lady Elizabeth!"

After a long silent dinner, Caroline was ready to turn in for the night. The curious thing was, her hammock was missing. When Byron entered the cabin, he chuckled at her curiosity, "Captain, my hammock.."

"Has been removed. After that little stunt you pulled this morning, you will be sleeping in my bunk. With me."

Her mouth dropped, "Sir, I...."

"Do not have a say in the matter."

She was on the verge of tears, "But why?"

Byron slowly stepped to her beautiful pouty face, and stroked her soft cheek, "To protect you."

Her lip quivered, "Who is going to protect me from you?"

Byron's smile eased as he thought, "Good question."

****

Chapter 7

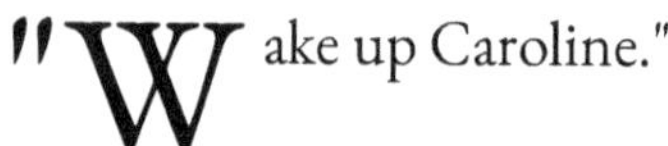

"Wake up Caroline."

Caroline moaned as someone gently shook her arm.

She carelessly yawned and stretched, "Good morning Captain. Sleep well?"

He was surprised by her pleasantness, "Shouldn't I be asking you?"

Caroline giggled, "Why yes, I did. Your bunk is extremely comfortable."

Byron smirked, "I slept well also. I love having another warm body next to me."

She couldn't contain her laugh, "Well there are twenty other men on this ship that wouldn't mind bunking with you due to comfort."

Byron's eyebrows raised with shock "Uuhhmm.. No."

She eased from the bed and pattered to the wash basin behind the dressing screen. Caroline then looked about the room for her dress but noticed it was missing, "Captain?!

Byron smiled as he adjusted his own clothes, "Yes Caroline?"

"My dress.. It seems to be missing."

She tried to cover herself the best she could as she heard his footsteps approaching, "It was soiled from you working. I have you a new one."

Caroline wrinkled her brow in confusion, "How did you know my measurements?"

He bit his lips as he looked at her figure, "Its not that hard to guess."

Her wrinkled brow turned into an angry glare, "You're insufferable."

Byron laughed a low seductive laugh, "Other woman would disagree."

"Did you sell them as well?"

His amusement quickly left his face. He could see pain in her eyes as she waited for his answer, "No."

"Well then, I would say them still having their freedom makes their opinion of you useless in this conversation." Carolines chest heaved with anticipation of his next blow.

Byron did not like the fact that she could easily put him in his place, "Oh Caroline, if you were only worth to be set free."

She pressed her eyes as tears streamed down her cheeks as he took his leave. She jumped as he slammed the door. Caroline crept from the screen and noticed her new stripped dress. When she finished dressing, she frowned as she looked in the mirror, "Damn him knowing a woman's anatomy." The dress fit her perfectly.

Byron roughly whispered to her as he escorted her off of the ship, "Do not make an attempt to escape. I will find you, and you do not want to know the consequences."

She looked down, "Yes sir."

Byron smirked at her gasp as he sat her on a dock post, "Now, Sam will be watching you. I expect a perfect drawing completed by the time I get back."

Caroline sighed as she looked to her sketch pad, "Yes sir."

Byron took a few steps away and turned back to her. She was the definition of adorable as she slightly pressed her tongue to the side of her mouth as she drew. She looked carefree and innocent. He had sever guilt of his harsh words earlier, "If only you were worth freeing." He knew he would regret it later.

"Byron! What brings you to Port Royal?"

Byron smirked as Shelby handed him a brandy, "Duke William, do you know of him?"

Shelby smirked, "Byron? What have you done?"

He leaned his head up and laughed, "Nothing yet. I was hired to kidnap his fiancé.."

She leaned her inquisitive brow to him, "But?.."

Byron turned his nervous chuckle to her, "Well.. Her little minx of a maid outsmarted me. They switched clothing."

She leaned back and cackled, "Oh my! You have truly ruined his plan!"

Byron's smile slowly disappeared, "His plan?"

Shelby's chuckle slowly stopped, "I've said too much.."

He leaned closer to his friend with his cold glare, "Tell me!"

She gulped loudly, "She was the one he wanted. Caroline is Elizabeth's half illegitimate sister. Her mother was the love of Elizabeth's father life.

Elizabeth's mother couldn't stand it, so when Carolines mother died, Elizabeth's mother made her life a living Hell."

Byron couldn't believe what he was hearing, "You're lying." He eased off of the sofa to take his leave, but stopped when Shelby spoke, "The back of her neck, check it; she was branded by Elizabeth's mother. It's their family crest."

Byron barely looked over his shoulder to her. He huffed and took his leave. All he could think about was to get back on the ship and to keep Caroline under lock and key. He had to find out Duke Williams intentions for her.

Caroline smiled as she finished her drawing. She did a double take as she noticed the young sailor that she met in the serving line and some of the other sailors as they were congratulating him on "becoming a man"; they had just returned from a brothel. Her smile turned into a slight frown as they locked eyes. She snapped out of his daze and buried herself into her drawing. She nervously cut her eyes to his feet as he stood in front of her.

Duncan nervously cleared his throat, "Hello Caroline."

She kept drawing, "Hello Duncan."

He shyly smiled, "You know my name?"

"Yes."

He was ecstatic, "How? Why?"

Caroline carelessly shrugged, "I asked."

Duncan lightly touched her hand. She slowly looked up to him, "Why did you want to know?"

"I liked you."

His smile eased, "Liked?"

Caroline sighed as she looked around the dock, "Yes.. Liked.."

Duncan was instantly hurt, "What..?"

She cut a cold smile, "How did you enjoy becoming a man?"

He leaned back to study her expression and shook his head, "She meant nothing. The Captain said that you were off limits. But I hear you sleep in the same chamber? How can you judge me?"

Caroline tilted her head and pressed her eyes, "He has not touched me. No one has."

Duncan breathed heavily as he shook his head, "I would like to court you if.."

"I'm afraid that would not be allowed. Let's not waste each other's time." She went back to her drawing, "Goodbye Duncan."

He growled as he boarded the ship. He looked down on her once he reached the deck. He studied her as he thought of a plan to rescue her, she would then be his then.

Chapter 8

As Caroline continued to wait for the captain to return, she smiled at a young girl about the age of five. She had thick kinky golden curls and blue eyes. Carolines eyes scanned the dock but did not see her guardian anywhere. She eased down to her level, "Hello."

The little girl giggled as she blushed, "Hello."

Caroline smiled a warm smile, "Where are your parents?"

The little girl carelessly shrugged and giggled. Caroline decided to keep her here in her eyes view until someone came looking for her.

After fifteen minutes had past, an older woman that was out of breath came running up to them, "Oh thank heavens! Marie, I told you not to run off like that!" She turned a cocked eyebrow to Caroline, "Thank you my dear. What is your name so I may tell the master."

Caroline gulped her nerves down, "My name?" She cut her eyes over to the dock entrance and noticed Byron talking to a blonde overly friendly woman.

The woman turned to see where her attention was drawn away and scowled, "Oh, so you're a woman of ill repute?"

Caroline gasped, "No ma'am! I..."

The woman cut her off, "Come Marie!" The woman roughly grabbed the little girls hand and lead her away.

As Byron continued to flirt with the women, Carolines face snapped to a noise from above, "Watch out below! The line is slipping!"

Byron turned his attention to a running Caroline. His brow wrinkled as he heard something snap. There was a woman yelling, "What tha!" Then a loud boom of a heavy crate falling through the old dock.

Byron pushed through the crowd, "Caroline? Caroline?!"

Little Marie was crying as she pointed down the massive hole in the dock. Byron quickly removed his dress jacket and jumped in.

Caroline was frantically trying to swim to the waters surface, but was stuck. Her ankle was also in sever pain. Byron eased down to her as she raised her finger tips, she could feel the surface on the other side as though it was taunting her. Byron swam in front of her and rolled his eyes. He quickly took out his knife and cut part of her dress which he thought was holding her down. When he tried to pull her up she wouldn't budge. He looked at her confused and tried again. Byron then pulled himself down to the crates bottom and noticed her ankle was stuck between the dock and heavy crate. He was starting to panic. He tried to move it but it was too heavy. He kept trying but it was no use. Byron swam back up to her pain stricken face. Caroline surprised him by placing her little hand on his cheek and patted it. It was as though she was telling him, it was alright. He shook his head as her eyes drifted closed. He lightly shook her but no response. He gasped for air as he screamed from the hole. Sam was already taking his jacket off to help. The two men pressed against the massive object and it barely moved. Byron quickly moved her ankle from its prison and headed to the surface. Duncan reached down and pulled the pale beauty from the water. Byron leaned over her and pressed on her chest. The cruel woman and little Marie stood in the crowd as they prayed for a miracle. Byron's heart began to sink as he continued his chest compressions, her lips were so blue and her skin white. He gasped for joy as she stared to spit salt water from her mouth. He quickly scooped her up and carried her on board the ship to get her warm. The cruel woman looked down to Marie with tears. If it not been for the sweet young lady, they both could be dead.

Chapter 9

Caroline had awoken with a startling gasp. She frantically breathed as she took in her surroundings. She then felt the ship move and realized that they were back at sea. As Caroline tried to shift to sit up, she hissed through her teeth from pain in her ankle. She wrenched when she pulled back the covers to see it badly bruised. Byron sighed as he quickly entered the cabin, he paused as he noticed Caroline was finally awake, "Hello."

Her lip quivered as she spoke, "The woman?! Marie?! Are they?!"

Byron eased down on the side of the bed and placed both hands on her shoulders, "Calm yourself.. They are fine."

Caroline pressed her eyes closed with relief, "Thank heavens."

Byron was puzzled by her, "Why did you do it?"

Caroline wrinkled her brow as she looked down, "I... I don't know.."

He gently grasped her little hand and gave her a sympathetic smile, "Its nice to see such bravery."

She shyly pulled her hand away, "I wasn't brave. I didn't have time to think."

Byron slightly pursed his lips, "Caroline, how did Lady Elizabeth's mother treat you?"

Caroline slowly raised her hand to the back of her neck as she stared in a daze, "She was a good mistress, why do you ask?"

He felt saddened by the fact Shelby was possibly right, "May I see the back of your neck?"

Her eyes locked to his as they were about to spill over with tears, "Why do you need to see my neck?"

Byron bit the bullet and pressed harder, "Caroline, have you been branded?"

Her lip quivered, "Who told you?"

He eased closer to her shaking form, "I'm so sorry."

Carolines eyes filled with anger, "Why do you pity me now? I begged you to believe me before, but you were blinded by your arrogance."

Byron made sure to keep his temper in check, he knew he deserved her harsh words, "I.. You're right. I did miss judged you." He continued to look at her with sympathy as he thought, "I will not tell her of her supposed father. If I could just see her neck." He would wait for tonight as she slept, then he could be sure. "Can I get you anything?"

Caroline kept her eyes locked on her lap as she shook her head, "No thank you."

He sighed as he continued to study her sad face, "I'm very pleased with the ships drawing, I just need you to sign it." He eagerly tried to hand her the paper.

Carolines eyes frantically looked around on her lap as she tried to think, "Sign? Oh no.." She bravely cleared her throat, "Captain, I am still very tired. May I please sign it another time?"

Byron's smile slowly disappeared, "Of course. I just wanted to make sure people knew it was your work."

She bit her lip to hold back her tears, "It doesn't matter. It's just a drawing."

He lightly turned her face to him with his finger tips, "Why would you say that? Other men would pay good money to have this done for them."

Caroline rolled her eyes and turned away from his gaze, "Pity, if only I could draw well enough to buy my freedom, but it is as you said; if I was only worth freeing."

Byron slowly hung his head as he eased from the bed. He quietly walked to his chart table and laid the drawing down. He turned back to her little form with sad eyes. She had turned away in the fetal position as she acted to be asleep again. Only, she was pressing her eyes closed to fight back her painful tears.

Later that night, Byron had slipped her some laudanum in her tea. The purpose was mostly because of her ankle, but it was also much easier to examine her neck without disturbing her. His hands slightly shook as he eased back her beautiful thick reddish brown hair. He pressed his eyes after they fell on a family crest that had been burned into her soft perfect skin.

Chapter 10

Byron smirked as Caroline yawned and stretched, "Good morning."

She cocked him a questionable look, "Good morning. Why are you so cheerful?"

"I have a new dress for you. It seems you're having trouble not ruining them lately." He strolled over and opened a box with ribbon.

Caroline eyes widened with excitement but her questionable look reappeared, "Where did you get it? How long have I been asleep?"

Byron slightly pursed his lips, "A day in a half. I purchased it from a merchant ship that we intercepted."

"Purchased or took it without asking?"

He chuckled as he slowly stepped to her bedside, "Why that's stealing dear Caroline! And I would never place stolen merchandise on your fair skin."

She sat shocked and speechless as she looked over her new dress, "Thank you. It is lovely."

She didn't look at Byron as he spoke and tucked a lose strand of hair behind her ear, "I thought the blue would go well with the color of your hair."

Caroline finally had the courage to look to his eyes, "Why are you being so kind?"

Byron bit his bottom lip, "I have a proposal. I am going to let you earn your freedom."

She slowly eased her posture up, "How?"

He gave a low seductive chuckle, "Not in my bed. I want you to draw the crew, so their family or loved ones will have a portrait of them while at sea."

Caroline had a shy smile spread across her lips, "Really? How many men?"

"Twenty five, including myself."

Her smile slowly disappeared, "How will I know that you will honor our agreement?"

Byron sighed as he walked over to his desk and pulled out a parchment, "Its all right here."She wrinkled her brow and bit her lip as he offered it to her. He was confused by her not receiving it, "What is wrong?"

She looked up with tear filled eyes, "Can you please read it to me?"

His expression turned to shock and sympathy, "Can you not read?" Caroline turned away as she shook her head. He felt terrible for his discovery, but her not signing her work made perfect sense now. With Lady Elizabeth's mother hating the poor girl, she wanted to make sure she had no chance of a suitable husband. How could she be so cruel to her? "Caroline, don't cry. Please. I will add in the contract that I shall be your teacher. How is that?"

Caroline snapped her tear soaked cheeks to him, "You will teach me to read?"

He gave a warm smile as he grasped her hand, "Of course. Now get dressed and we will get started on both today."

"How should I sign it?"

Byron widened his smile, "Just mark a x."

Caroline took the inked pen and made her mark.

Byron smiled at her and took place the document in his personal safe, "I will give you privacy to get dressed, unless you need assistance."

Her face quickly shot to his, "No thank you, I can manage."

Byron chuckled a low laugh as he took his leave. Caroline sighed deeply as she eased from the bed and prepared herself for the day. She couldn't help but wonder if he was going to be another disappointment in her life. So many people had let her down, why would he be any different?"

For the next two four hours, Caroline had managed to draw three portraits for the crewmen. As she sat on the deck, she would study her subject as they worked. Unfortunately, she did not know that she was being watched by Duncan as his thoughts ran through his head, "If only I could speak to her in private. The captain knew I wanted to help her escape, now he seems to be the hero. I will get my chance with her. Sooner or later." His blood boiled as he watched the captain leaned over her shoulder as she drew. Caroline turned her smile up to him as she showed him the drawing. Duncan almost began to shake with anger as the captain scooped her up due to her painful ankle and carried her to his cabin so they could start her reading lesson. "Bastard, you'll get what's coming to you soon."************

Chapter 11

Caroline watched as Byron moved about the cabin as he collected the materials for their lesson. She softly chuckled to herself as she watched his brow wrinkled as he looked about the room. She couldn't help but noticed that he was handsome.

Byron did a double take to her smiling expression, his own smile spread across his lips, "You're amused?"

Caroline shyly looked at her hands that were resting on the table, "No, not at all. Just eager to learn."

Byron continued to smile as he sat next to her, "Alright then. Here is a children's book that I learned from when I was a young boy. First we start off with our individual letters."

Her eyebrows peeked up as her eyes followed the movement of his hand. Caroline shyly smiled as she took the pen from him and placed it in her hand. She couldn't but noticed how close he had scooted next to her to watch. When she was practicing letter G in cursive, she sighed as she was having difficulty.

She blushed as Byron took her hand in his and guided her motions, "See, simple. Let's try it again. " She held her breath as he gently guided her hand again but noticed that he had placed his other on the side of her waist. As she was writing the letter, he gently released the hand that was guiding her but kept the other securely around her.

Caroline turned and smiled a proud smile to him when she finished writing the difficult letter. Her smile slowly disappeared when she noticed him looking at her lips.

Byron gently leaned in and kissed her softly. Caroline closed her eyes from the soft sensation. When he pulled away as he stroked her cheek, he found her looking puzzled, "What's the matter?"

She bit her lip and wrinkled her brow, "Did I.." He showed eagerness for her question, "Did I do that correctly?"

He chuckled, "Your letter?"

She slowly shook her head with worry, "No.. Did I kiss you properly?"

Byron continued to stroke her cheek with questionable eyes, "I.. was that your first?"

The look of worry grew on her sweet face, "Yes.."

Byron's chest heaved with lust as he leaned in and spoke against her lips, "Yes, but let's make sure I kissed you properly."

Caroline breathed in his kiss as he pressed hard against her full lips. She slightly whimpered as he pulled her to him by her waist. When he heard her muffled cry he reluctantly released her for air. "I'm sorry. I didn't hurt you did I?"

She shyly looked down as he studied her, "No sir."

He started to lean again but stopped as he watched her press her eyes closed, "What is wrong?"

Caroline kept her gaze forward, "I thought you were teaching me?"

Byron smirked as he studied her shyness, "I am. Shall we continue?"

As Caroline tried to concentrate, worry eased into her mind, "Will I still have to bunk with him? Does he expect more since I let him kiss me?"

After an hour of Byron instructions, he reluctantly left her to practice on her own. While on deck, his mind was constantly going back to his cabin.

*****************After a pleasant meal, Carolines nerves were making her stomach do summersaults. She tried to pretend that she was asleep when he came in, but he could tell otherwise, "Caroline?"

She peeked her eyes open to him, "Yes?"

"Can you please slide over? Your taking up most of my side."

Caroline gulped as she slid over to her side and watched as he climbed in. She waited for him to make his move but he just laid there in silence and studied her features. She bit her lip and sighed, "Are you not tired?"

Byron eased a sneaky smile across his lips, "No, why do you ask?" Caroline tried to think of a innocence answer but was interrupted by him, "I hope your not getting any crazy ideas. Just because I kissed you, doesn't mean you can take advantage of me."

She chuckled and shook her head as she turned away, "Please forgive my impure thoughts. I will try to control myself throughout the night."

Byron turned to her and pulled her back close to him, "I'm not going to try anything. I just want to hold you."

Caroline looked over her shoulder to his lustful eyes. She pressed her closed as he leaned in and kissed her for a few seconds and pulled his lips away. He whispered against them, "Goodnight."

She turned her face back away and sighed with a smile, "Goodnight."****
****

Chapter 12

Caroline had nervous butterflies in her stomach as Duncan plopped down in front of her for his portrait. She pressed a fake smile across her lips, "Hello Duncan."

"Hello Caroline. My, that's a lovely new dress you're wearing."

Caroline pressed her eyes on her sketch pad, "Thank you."

"What did you have to do to get it?"

She eased her angry eyes to him, "What do you mean?"

Duncan smiled and evil smile to her, "How many times did you spread your legs for him to thank him for it?"

Caroline felt shame as she turned her sad eyes back to her drawing, "Why are you saying such cruel things?"

"What? Can't stand the truth?"

She had tears ease down her cheeks, "But.. it's not."

Duncan did feel bad for saying his lies, but if it was the only way to keep her out of the captains arms, then so be it, "Perhaps, but the crew thinks other wise."

Caroline then noticed Duncan's eyes widened with fear. She held her breath when she heard Byron's voice behind her, "What are you two talking about?"

Caroline slowly eased her tear soaked face to him, "Im not feeling well today. May I please draw tomorrow?"

Byron pressed his teeth as he looked to a frightened Duncan, "What did you bloody say to her?"

Duncan lept from his seat as he charged to him, "Only the truth! We all know she's spread her legs for ya!"

Byron snatched Carolines sketch pad from her hands and drew something quickly, "Your portrait is finished! How do you like it?"

Duncan's eyes widened further as Byron showed him a stick figure hanging by a noose, "Why, that looks nothing like me."

Byron charged towards him, "Sure it does. Let me show ya."

The crew stepped back as he lunged and grabbed Duncan by the throat. He feverishly punched him until Sam told him it was enough. He then dragged him to a frightened Caroline, "Now apologize!"

Duncan heaved as he glared up at her, "I'm sorry.."

Byron shook him, "Louder!"

He pressed his eyes as he screamed, "Sorry!"

Byron then slung him to Sam, "Lock him up until our next stop! Bread and water only!"

Caroline gasped as an angry Byron was about to scoop her up to carry her, but she stopped him, "No Captain! Please. I can walk, it doesn't hurt as much."

Byron's expression eased as he offered her his arm. She smiled a shy smile as she took it. The crew looked upon her with sympathetic eyes as she limped to their cabin.

Once inside she turned to a sad Byron. He slowly stepped to her and cupped her face, "Please, don't listen to him. He is angry that he cannot have you. I have not said a word about anything that has happened between us."

She gently placed her hand on one of his and stroked it with her thumb, "I believe you."

He smiled as he gently leaned in and kissed her. Caroline gladly accepted it. He whispered against her lips, "We can still do your lesson today."

She eased a smile as she looked at his full lips, "Yes please."

Caroline eagerly watched as Byron showed her how to write her name, "Now your turn." He watched as she bit her bottom lip and studied what he had written before. She softly said each letter as she wrote it. As he watched her lips slowly moving, he moved to her neck as though in a trance and gently kissed it. Caroline pressed her eyes from the sensation. Byron gently turned her face to him and feverishly kissed her plump lips and pulled her closer. She placed her hands on both sides of his face as he kissed her. When his mouth went back to her neck, her brow wrinkled at the sensation of his fingertips on the bare flesh that was right above her garters. As they traveled closer to her intimate area, she gasped and stopped his hand, "No Byron! Please!"

He immediately stopped and leaned away, "I'm sorry. I.."

Caroline looked down to hide her flushed face, "I'm sorry too. It did feel nice, but.."

He gently grabbed her hand, "You don't have to be. I shouldn't have. You're just so beautiful, I couldn't control myself, but it won't happen again unless you want it to."

She turned a shy smile to him, "I know you wouldn't hurt me. I wish I could be more accepting, but I.."

Byron stroked her cheek, "Please don't regret your morals. You will make a fine, loyal wife someday."

She looked down, "That's why I can't. Not until.."

He then felt something growling inside himself as he thought, "Marriage? What farmer or clerk deserves you? No one!"

His temper eased as she looked back up to his sad face, "Are you alright?"

Byron rubbed the tip of his nose against hers, "Never better."

Chapter 13

Byron paused as he stepped into the moonlit cabin. Caroline was sitting on the edge of the bed deep in thought. She noticed his presence and turned a smile to him, "I promise not to take advantage of you."

He bit his lip and chuckled, "Thank you for respecting my boundaries. I can now sleep better now, knowing that."

Caroline giggled as she scooted back on the bed and eased under the covers. Her mouth went dry when she watched him remove his shirt, "Captain?"

He smirked and shook his head, Don't worry, it's just warmer tonight than usual."

Caroline quietly nodded and gently laid down. She eagerly watched as he eased under the bed sheets and pulled her to him. Her eyes scanned over his chiseled chest. She wrinkled her brow as she felt something fluttering in the pit of her stomach. Byron quietly studied her, he sighed as he grasped her hand and placed it in his warm bare chest. She slightly gasped at the warmth that was radiating from him, "You're so warm."

He leaned closer and kissed her forehead, "And you're so soft." Byron then kissed her eyelids, then her lips, down to her neck. He lingered there for a moment then bravely eased the shoulder off of her chemise and placed his lip on her firm breast. Caroline's eyes flew open as she cried out in a whimper "Byron.. no.. I..."

He leaned back over her, "I won't do anything that could jeopardize your wedding night."

She bit her lip, "But, how will you get pleasure out of it?"

His devilish grin spread across his lips, "I want to only pleasure you." He kissed her neck again, "Please.""Byron, I don't know.." she leaned her head back as he continued his seduction.

He smiled against her inner thigh as he nipped at her soft flesh. Her light sighs taunted him to do more. Byron moaned as he tasted her between her folds. Caroline gasped and bucked against his mouth. He loved how her soft legs felt against his bare shoulders as he continued to taste her. She pushed her words through the mind numbing sensation, "Byron? I.. I.."

His tongue eased deeper as her legs began to shake and stiffen. Byron smiled to himself as he felt her fluid gush from its prison for the first time. He quietly thought, "She's mine now. She won't be able to have another man touch her after this."

Caroline sighed deeply as her orgasim high eased. Her eyes grew heavy as she noticed him leaning over her smiling, "What have you done?"

His smile slowly disappeared as he leaned down to kiss her, "I just wanted a taste, you are still a virgin." He watched as her brow wrinkled as she tried to process if she had done anything wrong. Byron felt sympathy for her questioning her innocence, "Caroline, you did nothing wrong. Please know that."

She stroked the side of his face with a sad expression, "Goodnight."

He leaned down and kissed her forehead, "Goodnight."

Caroline turned away and smiled as he pulled her to his warm bare chest. She knew she let him go too far, but she couldn't say no. She actually respected and admired him.

Byron stroked her long beautiful hair as he noticed her breathing was deep since she had fallen asleep. He was actually proud of himself for not taking full advantage of her. He would not have been able to forgive himself if he had. She trusted him, and with her being his student, she looked up to him. Byron then started to think about what would happen if the Duke found her, or after she gained her freedom, would she want to stay without marriage. Of course not, she just had her first sexual experience and obviously enjoyed it. Other men would try to do more with her if he didn't stop them. He slightly growled as he pictured the Duke forcing her in his bed. It made his blood boil. He had made his decision, she would be his, he just had to find a way of securing it.

****

Chapter 14

Caroline smiled as they eased into Charlestown harbor. There were flocks of small parakeets flying about in the sunny sky. She couldn't wait to have the opportunity to draw them. Byron stood behind the helm as he watched her innocent expression. He couldn't wait to give Caroline a tour of her new home. Finally after securing the ship, Byron escorted Caroline to their carriage.

She was starting to wonder why he brought her here. She kept her thoughts to herself as she leaned and looked out the window. Caroline wrinkled her brow as Byron leaned over her and eased down the carriage window shade. She turned her sad pouty expression, "Why..?"

She didn't have time to finish her sentence before he had his lips pressed to hers. He feverishly kissed her neck as he held her to him. With her eyes closed she sighed, "Byron, where are we going?"

Byron spoke against her flesh, "I'm taking you to my plantation. I'm going to show you your new home."

Caroline squeaked as she pushed him off of her, "What?! But you said that I have earned my freedom."

Byron smirked, "And you have, but I was not just going to drop you off all by yourself without any protection."

She looked down as she tried to take in what he said, "I have to warn Lady Elizabeth."

She turned her sad gaze to Byron as she heard him growl, "Lady Elizabeth is about to be wed. She is fine."

Caroline leaned her sad expression to him and stroked his cheek, "Please, I have to know she is alright."

Byron's temper eased as he looked into her sadness, "How can I say no to you? I will find out what happened, but I do not want the Duke knowing where you are just yet."

She studied his sincereness, "Why? What do you know?"

He leaned in against her lips , "I promise I will tell you when the time is right. I haven't broken my word yet, have I?"

She smiled before she kissed him, "No, I trust you."

Caroline gasped at the sight of Grace Hall, "Byron! She is lovely!"

He leaned over her shoulder and whispered in her ear, "That's why you belong here. I like beautiful things."

She bit her lip as she took in the sight of the beautiful manicured grounds. As they approached the house she noticed a young beautiful pregnant lady waiting on the porch. Her heart sank as the wondered if she was another piece in his collection.

She gulped as Byron helped her from the extravagant carriage, and escorted her to the woman, "Caroline, met my younger sister Abigail."

Caroline smiled as the woman offered her hand to shake, "Caroline! It is so nice to meet you! Please do come in. I have lunch waiting on the back veranda."

Byron sat and studied Caroline and Abigail as they easily conversed. He silently prayed that she would want to stay. The party then turned their attention to footsteps on the porch, "Hello Gregory! I was wondering what my sister had done with you."

Gregory gave a warm smile and shook his hand, "You should know I'm the only man tough enough to handle your dear sister."

Abigail pursed her lips as Gregory leaned down and kissed her cheek, "Tread lightly dear." Abigail turned her attention to Caroline, "Caroline, met my husband Gregory Drayton."

Caroline and Gregory both exchanged smiles and nods.

Abigail sighed as she stood, "Byron, why don't you give Caroline a tour of the grounds while I have her room prepared."

Byron quickly stood and whispered in his sitter's ear, "Put her in the blue room."

Abigail smirked, "Any particular reason brother?"

Byron just chuckled as he kissed his sisters brow. He then turned to Caroline and offered her his arm, Come my dear."

Caroline bit her lip as she walked across the ornate bridge. She leaned over as she looked into the water to see her reflection. Her eyes then turned to Byron's as he towered behind her, "What do you think?"

She shyly blushed as she turned to him, "I think it's all so lovely."

He leaned in and placed his hands on both sides of her waist. He lingered for a short moment over her lips then kissed her. Caroline moaned as she wrapped her arms around his neck. Byron hoped that his home would be enough to keep her, but knew better. He knew she would eventually want a husband and children, he pondered if she would consider him for a husband.

After a long walk in the Charlestown heat, Abigail smiled as she showed Caroline to her room. She was puzzled by her expression, "Do you not like it?"

Caroline had eyes almost full of tears, "No, it's beautiful."

Chapter 15

----

* ***** Authors note*******"Please know, even though I am from the south, I do not approve of past slavery. As beautiful as the plantations were, unfortunately most of them survived with slaves. Again, I do not approve of what my ancestors did, but it is unfortunately part of history. "**********************************

The party was enjoying their evening meal as the head house slave stepped through the dining hall. Abigail smiled, "What is it Peter?"

The man nervously cleared his throat, "Ma'am, their is a Miss Sylvia here to see Master Byron."

Byron sighed and pressed his eyes and shook his head, "I told that banshee to stay away." He then looked to a nervous Caroline, "Make her wait outside, maybe the mosquitoes will carry her away."

Peter chuckled, "Yes sir."

Abigail frowned at her brother, "Byron, is that any way to treat a lady?"

"Lady?! She is no lady! She is a lying vile.." he stopped as he noticed Carolines expression turned sadder. He rolled his eyes and eased from the table, "Very well."

Byron sighed as he gently closed the front door, "Why are you here Sylvia?"

The tall blonde strolled over to him and wrapped her arms around his neck, "Is that anyway to treat your past lover? I heard that you were home and I thought we could be friends again."

Byron pulled her arms from around his neck, "I haven't forgotten the fact that I caught you with two men at once. I was a fool to think you could be faithful."

Caroline eased to the window as she listened as Sylvia spoke, "I also heard you brought a woman home with you, is she your mistress?"

Byron strolled away from her, "That is none of your concern."

"So she means nothing to you?"

He quickly snapped his gaze to her, "I didn't say that. Again, none of your concern, not get off of my property!"

Sylvia sneered at him, "Good riddance."

Byron scoffed as he watched her enter her Carriage. He turned back to the house but as he did he noticed the parlor curtain move. He quickly entered the house and entered the dark room, "Caroline, come out."

Caroline bit her lip as she eased up from behind the couch, "I'm.. "

Byron smiled, "An ease dropper."

She blushed as she stared up to him, "I'm sorry.. I.."

"Was jealous?"

Caroline slowly nodded, "She's very pretty."

He eased his hand up and stroked her cheek, "Not quite as pretty as you though."Caroline sighed at his compliment. "Why don't we turn in for the night?"

She chuckled, "I'm sorry, but I have no proper reason to keep you warm tonight."

He leaned down and whispered in her ear, "Perhaps I can sneak in your room later?"

"I think I'll lock my door."

He raised his eyebrows to her confident smirk, "Dear oh dear, I think you've got me."

Caroline cocked a questionable eyebrow to him, "I guess I do."

He chuckled a low seductive laugh and offered her his arm.

Later that night, Caroline laid wide awake as she tried to fall asleep. She sighed as she thought about how much colder her bed was. She held her breath as thought she heard a noise. She sat up as Byron appeared from behind a secret passage behind the fireplace, "Byron, what are you doing?" She became speechless as he stood before her and completely undressed. She eased away from him as he approached her bedside. She was trembling as he reached for her cheek. She exhaled a shaking breath as he eased to her and whispered, "I always sleep like this in Charlestown. Ya know, because it's warmer."

Caroline gulped as she tried to keep her eyes on his face, "But won't it be warmer next to me?"

Had chuckled as he looked at her lips, "Im willing to make that sacrifice to keep you warm."

She was speechless as he eased into her bed. He gently eased her down and laid facing her. Caroline bit her lip as she leaned up on her elbow and then kissed him. Byron moaned as she eased closer to him. She swallowed her fear as her hand slowly traveled down to his lower abdomen and found his stiff member. He gasped while popping his eyes open to hers as she stroked him. He leaned his head away slightly as he closed his eyes again, "What are you doing?"

Caroline kissed his neck as she continued to stroke him, "I want to pleasure you, am I doing it properly?"

Byron growled through pressed teeth as he was getting close to his release, "Yes..." He kept his eyes closed as he pulled her night gown over her head to feel her soft skin against his. Caroline gasped and moaned from his body heat. Byron eased his eyes open as he studied her body, "You're so exquisite."Caroline smiled against his lips as she kept up her pace. She could tell he was getting close as he grew stiffer in her hand. He leaned his head back as he grabbed her night gown and covered his excitement as he climaxed. He tossed the garment to the floor and leaned over her. She breathed heavily as his hand traveled down between her legs and gently slipped in and out. Caroline slightly open her mouth and leaned her head back. She watched as he took one breast into his mouth as he kept stroking her core. When he move his lips right above hers, his expression was so intense and freighting. She grabbed both sides of his head and pulled him to her pouty lips. Byron had a hard time to keep his lust under control. He wanted to plunge into her depths but shook it from his mind. He leaned up and smiled at her stressed expression, "I love you." She was shocked but, couldn't say anything since her breathing became labored as she came on his fingers. She was shocked as he placed them in his mouth and sucked her juices from them.

Caroline studied his handsome face and whispered, "I love you too". She squeaked as he pulled her to him. She nuzzled into his neck and fell asleep.

Chapter 16

Byron chuckled as he kissed Caroline goodbye before heading into town, "No, I shall not be all day. I promised you I would take you on your first picnic remember?"

She cocked a questionable brow, "Why cannot I go with you? You're not hiding anything from me are you?"

He bit his lip as he stroked her chin, "Like I said, I will tell you when the time is right."

She pouted as he kissed her forehead and mounted his horse with Gregory beside him, "Stay close to the house until I return."

"Yes sir." She turned to a beaming Abigail, "What is so amusing?"

"I don't think I have ever seen Byron so publicly affectionate. Or patience. It's amazing."

Caroline's brow wrinkled, "Oh? But.. never mind."

Abigail stepped to her, "What is it?"

She slightly blushed, "I know he has had previous women, has he ever brought them here before?"

Abigail chuckled as she shook her head, "No my dear, you must be very dear to his heart to bring you here to meet me."

Caroline blushed as she looked down, "I think very highly of your brother."

Abigail took her arm into hers, "I know he feels the same about you. Now come inside." Caroline smiled as she ushered her in.

*************Gregory and Byron slowly trotted into town. Byron's first destination was his lawyers office to tie down any word on Lady Elizabeth's marriage and the Dukes possible location. It turned out that his lawyer had unearthed more information on Carolines past. Byron was shocked to find out the true reason the Duke wanted Caroline instead. Her farther had left his entire estate to her on his death bed. His lawyer had sent word to several of the law offices along the coast, all the way up to Boston. Caroline was a wealthy woman and did not even know it. As for Elizabeth's dowery, she was left with fifteen thousand pounds and nothing more since her marriage was secured. Byron was grateful that that Carolines father cared enough to leave her very comfortable, but that did not keep him from hating him for what he had done in his past. Their next stop was the Saint Fury. Sam was giving him the run down on the ships repairs and crew.

Byron froze as he mentioned Duncan had been released in the city, "When did you release him?"

Sam shrugged a day ago? Why do you ask?"

Byron leaned over the railing to Gregory, "Ready the horses now!" He sprinted down to the dock and jumped on his horse. Gregory was shocked as he took off without warning.

Caroline slowly walked on the massive porch as she fanned herself from the summer heat. Abigail was upstairs resting due to her pregnancy. As she turned the corner to the front porch she gasped as Duncan slowly stepped up to her. Her mouth went dry as she wrinkled her brow, "Duncan, what are you doing here?"

Duncan smirked as he walked past her and studied the massive house while he whistled, "My.. my.. this is beautiful." He then turned to her, "Just like you."

Caroline tried to keep calm until there was a roll of thunder, she looked up to the dark sky and prayed for Byron to show up any moment, "Duncan please tell me what is it you seek?"

Duncan seemed to have pain in his eyes, "I just wanted to tell you, I'm sorry for the mean things I said, and that you can leave with me. He won't be able to find us."

She took a small step back, "Duncan, I'm not leaving. I lo..."

He growled as she was about to finish her sentence, "Love?! Ha! That bastard doesn't love you! He's just after your money!"

Caroline furiously shook her head with worry, "Wha..? What are you talking about?"

Duncan was on the verge of tears, "Your Lady Elizabeth's half sister! Your father left you everything!"

She was now crying, "Who told you this?! You lie!"

Duncan touched her cheek, "No, I overheard two lawyers in a pub! Come with me! I can save you from him!"

Caroline tried to pull away from his grasp but he growled as she fought, "Stop! I know what's best for us! Stop fighting me!" He growled one final time and lost his temper. He roughly shoved her down, but as he did; Caroline reached for something to stop her fall. Duncan's eyes widened as she lost her footing and fell on the front brick steps hitting her head in the process. Duncan quickly stepped down to the unconscious beauty and lifted her head. He cried as he felt something warm and wet on his hand. It was shaking as he lifted it to his face and noticed it was covered in bright red blood, "Oh, dear God."

Byron thundered into the scene with his horse galloping at full speed. He jumped down and ran to him and screamed, "What have you done?! Oh, God! What have you done..?" He quickly shoved him away and cradled Carolines limp body. Oliver and Abigail had heard the commotion and ran to fetch the doctor. Gregory pressed his teeth as he stomped to Duncan. Duncan panicked and retreated in the woods. Gregory did chased after him, but lost his trail.

Later that night Byron squeezed Carolines hand as he silently prayed for her to wake. All he could think about was revenge. He growled as he pushed from the bedside and packed for his journey. Abigail begged him not to go, but she couldn't reason with him. He kissed Carolines soft lips as a tear eased out of his eye. He then took his leave to hunt down Duncan and make him pay.

Chapter 17

Carolines eyes slowly blinked as she wrinkled her brow. She waved her hand in front of her face, but all she saw was a faint shadow. She started to hyperventilate as she threw off her covers and jumped from the bed. Her lips quivered as she placed her shaking hands in front of her as she tried to feel her way through the room. Caroline cried out when she tripped and fell onto the floor. Abigail and Gregory sprung into her room, "Caroline?! Oh my, what happened?"

Caroline started to scream and cry, "I can't see! I can't see!"

Abigail was in shock as she kneeled beside her and hugged her, "Sshh.. I'm here.. Ssshh.."

Caroline now was whimpering, "I can't.."

Gregory sent Oliver to fetch the doctor. After his examination, he pulled Abigail and Gregory to the side and spoke in a low tone, "It seems her injury has caused her blindness. Rarely, it can correct its self, but I wouldn't get my hopes up." Abigail had tears ease down her cheeks as he continued, "Might I suggest an Asylum? With your condition, it would be difficult to.."

Abigail snapped up her hand with an angry glare, "What did you say?"

The doctor nervously cleared his throat and tried to speak to Gregory but Abigail interrupted, "Don't you dare turn your attention away from me! I'm head of this household while my brother is away! And we are most certainly not sending her to a God awful Asylum!"

Caroline softly spoke, "Yes you are."

Abigail charged to her bedside and held her cheek, "No! I won't! I will miss you too much, and you are supposed to help me when my baby comes."

Carolines lip quivered as she eased her shaking hand and found her cheek, "I will not be a burden to you or your brother."

Abigail shook her head, "He would never forgive me. I couldn't bare it!"

Caroline pressed her eyes and nodded, "I shall wait a little for Byron. If he doesn't return, then I shall leave."

The doctor nodded, "Very well." He then took his leave.

Abigail had a stern voice, "Caroline, what damned Asylum could teach you how to survive better than I?!"

Caroline was in shock, "What?!"

"You're blind, not deaf! I know you heard me!"Caroline was speechless as she continued, "I'm not giving up and neither should you! You're going to get out of this bed and learn this house inch by inch! Do you understand me?!"Caroline slightly nodded. "Good! I'll be back in fifteen minutes to assist you with your dress." Abigail closed the door and covered her mouth before a sob could escape. She quickly ran downstairs to the porch and let her ugly tears go as she cried for her dear friend. She hated saying those things to her, but she couldn't give up on her. She knew her brother wouldn't. She dried her tears as she heard Gregory approached, "Was I awful to say those things?"

Gregory took big steps to her and pressed his lips upon hers. He smiled as he pulled away to rub the tip of his nose against hers, "I love you dearly wife, no one else could have more love by speaking the harsh truth." Abigail leaned in and hugged him.

*******************Byron had been to sea for a long two months. He had finally caught up with Duncan's ship and forced her to run a ground. It was pouring rain as he found the coward shaking in the corner of the ships deck. Duncan stuttered as he lifted his shaking hands, "I'm sorry! I.. never meant to hurt her!"

Byron grabbed him by the collar, "You're about to look just like your portrait."

Duncan violently shook his head, "No! No! Please!"

Sam smiled as he swung the rope over the lower bow of the ship. Byron's steps thundered as he placed the rope around his neck and stepped back as Sam pulled him up. Duncan's feet kicked as he tried to breath. Byron had a sigh of relief knowing he could return home. He had more hope than dread that Caroline was okay.

****

Abigail groaned and stretched her back as she walked the houses massive porch. Her attention was drawn to an approaching carriage. She squinted her eyes and smiled as she realized it was her brother. Byron chuckled as he sprung from his seat and hugged his very pregnant sister. He beamed as he looked at her but his smile eased as Abigail's lip stared to quiver. Byron shook his head, "No."

He then noticed something on the corner of his eye. He slowly turned to Caroline as she walked on the porch, "Abigail?! Was that the Asylum carriage? Is it time to go?"

Byron turned an angry brow to his sister then back to Caroline. He swallowed his nervousness as he walked to her. Caroline paused as she heard unfamiliar footsteps approaching her, "Gregory? Is that you?"

Byron had a tear ease out of his eye as he noticed her fingertips fluttering against the porch railing, "Hello Caroline."

She paused as she gasped and covered her mouth, "Byron?"

He took slow steps to her and grasped her little hand, "I missed you terribly."

Caroline pressed her eyes as tears ease out.

*****************Did you like the chapter?

Will Carolines disability keep her from marriage?

What will Byron do?

Chapter 18

Byron gently ushered Caroline into the parlor and closed the door. He was amazed by the fact how well she glided to the couch and sat. He cleared his throat and strolled to her and sat. Caroline had a look of worry since he had yet to kiss her, "Did you find Duncan?"

Byron took in her figure as he answered her, "Yes." His fingers twitch to touch her, but he was afraid she may not feel the same as before.

She was about to speak, but there was a knock at the parlor door. Byron sighed from the interruption, "Enter."

A nervous Oliver appeared, "Miss Caroline, Ashton Henson is here to see you."

Caroline wrinkled her brow as she looked towards his voice, "Why?"

Oliver carelessly shrugged, "Don't know. Should I show him in?"

Abigail smirked as she entered the room, "Why yes Oliver. Byron, I think Ashton wanted to see Caroline in private."

Both Byron and Caroline snapped their faces to her. He huffed as he eased from the couch and left with Abigail. As they turned the corner he grabbed her arm to face him, "What the Hell are you doing? Leaving her in there alone with that bastard?"

Abigail couldn't contain her chuckle, "Why dear brother, I just did you a favor." Byron scoffed as she proceeded, "I just gave you the perfect reason to, how did you put it last time; to beat the ever loving shit out of him?"

Byron's eyes widened as he stepped back to the parlor and pressed his ear to the door.

Caroline nervously fanned herself as Ashton sat unusually close to her, "That is by far, the prettiest dress I've ever seen."

She rolled her eyes as she looked away. She could feel his eyes burning into her chest, "Thank you. Abigail dresses me, as though I'm her doll."

Ashton eased closer and caressed her arm, "When I saw you at the market in town, I couldn't get you out of my head."

Caroline shifted away, "How is Sylvia your fiancé?"

He smirked at her sarcasm, "Fine. Thank you for asking."

Caroline gasped as she felt his finger tips touch the top of her cleavage, "Stop!"

Ashton chuckled as he pressed down on her and kissed between her bosom.

She growled as she tried to push him off. Both of them looked to the door as Byron flung it opened it while holding a two by four. Ashton's eyes widened with fear, "Byron! I.. didn't realize you were home."

Byron stomped to Ashton and pulled him up by his fancy dress jacket. He tried to get his footing, but it was useless. As he turned around to face Byron after releasing him, he gulped as he saw the two by four about to collide with his face. Ashton was almost knocked out as he fell off the porch and tumbled down the stairs. Abigail snickered as she watched Byron beat Ashton black and blue. He then slung him back into his carriage and told the driver to leave.

As Byron approached a smiling Abigail he paused and shook his head at her amusement. He sighed as he entered the parlor to find a silent Caroline, "Are you alright?"

She nodded, "Yes, thank you."

He started to walk to the couch again but Oliver knocked on the door again. Byron roared, "What?!"

"Sir, the Watkins twins are here to see Miss Caroline."

Byron placed his hands on his hips as he spoke in Carolines direction, "Oh really?"

Byron picked up the board again and headed for the porch. Caroline flenched as she heard yelling and two loud thuds, then a loud groaning. She sat and listened as another carriage left. She jumped as she heard Byron's footsteps pounding on the wooden floor towards the parlor. She prepared for his anger and was right to do so. Abigail was following close behind him. Caroline jumped again as he barged through the door, "Why are all of these bloody idiots appearing on my doorstep to see you!?"

Caroline looked towards his direction as her lip quivered, "I don't know. I've only been in town a few times with Abigail."

Byron turned to Abigail, "Well?"

She crossed her arms in a challenge, "Well what?"

"Why are these men courting her?!"

Abigail chuckled a sarcastic laugh, "Brother! Look at her! Why would they not? Plus let's not forget that she is available since you have no understanding with her."

His expression eased as he looked at Caroline. She sniffled as tears fell from her eyes. Byron didn't turn his gaze away as he spoke to Abigail, "Leave us."She smirked as she turned away and softly closed the door.

Caroline looked up towards him as she heard Abigail leave. Byron sighed as he ran his hands through his hair, "Caroline, I'm sorry for scaring you. I was so angry about not being here to protect you, but that is my own fault. I felt helpless and I wanted to take my vengeance out on Duncan."

Caroline eased from the couch and stepped to him. Byron held out his hand and pulled her closer to him. Caroline smiled a sad smile, "I understand."

He gave her a puzzled look as she offered him her hand to shake it, "What? What is this?"

"Will you not shake hands with me? Is that not what friends do?" Her brow wrinkled with worry.

He tipped her chin and leaned her head up to his, "We are more than friends."

Caroline tried not to cry, "But what am I?"

He leaned in and spoke on her lips before pressing a kiss on her lips, "My everything."

*******************Did you like the chapter?

What will happen next?

Will they be married?

Chapter 19

Abigail gasped as Caroline turned around to face her in her wedding gown, "You're stunning! I can't wait for him to see you."

Caroline looked down and blushed, but her smile eased with worry, "I.. I hope he is not making a mistake. I know he loves the sea, and I feel terrible he will be selling the Saint Furry."

Abigail stroked her cheek, "Caroline, you are the most important thing to him. Don't ever believe or think your a mistake."

Caroline smiled to her direction with a lone tear trailing down her cheek. She then turned to a knock on the door. It was Oliver informing them that it was time. Abigail gently ushered her to Gregory as he waited at the back of the church. He tucked her arm in his and gave Abigail a kiss before the wedding march started. Abigail followed behind as her maiden of honor. Byron swallowed the lump in his throat as his beautiful bride approached him. He couldn't believe how blessed he was that she had survived her accident. Caroline had fought him on the matter, but he made sure that she knew, she was not a burden with her blindness. How could she ever be?

Caroline slightly tremble as Gregory gave her away to Byron. The ceremony was short and sweet, but a lavish party followed. Caroline nervously fidgeted with her fingers as Byron lead her to the dance floor for their first dance as man and wife. He leaned down and whispered in her ear, "Don't worry, I've got you." She smiled a deep sighed as he pulled her close to him as they glided through the ballroom. Other couples joined in.

Carolines chest heaved as she silently stood in Byron's bedroom. She was not familiar with the furniture arrangement and was afraid that she might bump into something. She held her breath as she heard the door open and closed. Byron gently spoke, "Its me." He took his time as he took in the view of her with her wedding dress on. He gently eased behind her and placed his fingertips on her shoulders and kissed her neck. Caroline tilted her head back in a sigh as he loosened the ribbons on the back of her dress.

Byron leaned back while biting his bottom lip with a smile as he loosened her corset next. Once it was loose enough he pulled all of the garments down, with the exception of her garters and thigh stockings. He tried to keep his breathing under control as he pulled his own shirt from his torso. Caroline slightly looked over her shoulder as he scooped her up from the pile of clothing on the floor. She pressed her eyes as he gently laid her down on his bed and could feel him staring at her naked form. He was slightly amused, but then realized how different this had to be since she could no longer see. He stroked her face as he laid on top of her and kissed her eye lids, "May I please see your eyes?"

Caroline hesitated but opened them for him, "Why?"

Byron smiled down on her, "Because, you're still beautiful. All of you."

She smiled as she melted into his kiss. He was trying to take his time, but two months at sea had taken its toll on his lust. His tongue parted her lips as he moaned into her mouth. Caroline whimpered as he moved to her neck as he nudged her legs open with his knee. As he continued to kiss her, she could feel him stripping the last of his clothing off to free himself. Without warning or hesitation, Byron moaned as he slipped in between her warmth. Caroline gasped loudly from the pain and threw her head backwards. Byron continued his slow strokes until the pain eased. Once he could feel her matching his thrust, he dug deeper into her. She could feel a familiar but stronger pulling sensation in the pit of her stomach. Byron bucked faster as she locked her legs around his bare backside. On the verge of her orgasim she cried out his name and dug her nails into his lower back. He felt her spasms around him and pressed his forehead into the mattress above her shoulder and moaned. Caroline smiled as she felt his release and felt complete.

****************Did you enjoy the chapter?

What will happen next?

Chapter 20

Caroline smiled as she felt the tall grass against her fingers while she walked across the vast field. She could see everything. In the distance on a hill, she could see a large school. It brought joy to her heart seeing it there. Caroline felt purpose and pride when she looked upon it. Her heart pounded with anticipation as she walked closer to her destination. Just as she is about to step on the porch step, she wakes up. Byron pulled her closer as he heard her startled breathing, "Bad dream?"

Caroline turned over to him and gently touched his face as her eyes focused past it, "No, it was wonderful."

He smiled as he eased his face closer to hers, "Was it about me?"

She couldn't contain her laugh, "Do you want the honest truth?"

Byron's eyebrows perked up, "Your not dreaming about someone else are you?"

Caroline leaned in and softly kissed him, "Your face is all that I see when I dream."

He smirked as he played with her hand, "What was your dream about?"

She pushed her lips to the side and shook her head, "Its hard to explain, but I think I will know later."

Byron kissed her forehead, his eyes then traveled to her plump lips. He leaned down and pressed his against them. Caroline moaned as he parted her lips with his tongue. She breathed deeply as his lips traveled to her neck as he settled over her. Byron was wondering if he was still asleep and dreaming when he looked down upon her, "I love you."

Caroline smiled as she wrapped her arms around his neck, "I love you too."

The later that afternoon, Caroline was surprised by Byron with a picnic. She was excited but also sad that she wouldn't be able to see the scenery. They took a small carriage ride to a lower part of the estate beside a small river. As Caroline sat on the blanket she could hear the water flowing, birds chirping, and smell wisterias blooming. It was perfect. Byron noticed the smile on her lips, "Why are you smiling?"

She turned her happy face in his direction, "This place seems lovely."

He was relieved to hear that she was enjoying their outing, "This was my favorite place as a boy."

"When did you and Abigail move here?"

Byron wrinkled his brow as the past crept into his mind, "I was ten. Abigail six."

Caroline could hear the sadness in his voice, "What happened?"

He stared at her sad sympathetic face, "My mother died in childbirth. My uncle found Abigail and I in an orphanage and brought us here."

Caroline swallowed a lump, "My father?"

His eyes widened with shock, "How did you..?"

She pressed her eyes closed at the memory of Duncan's words, "Duncan told me." Byron remained silent as he. clenched his jaw. "My father placed you in the orphanage didn't he?"

His tone was cold and flat, "Yes."

"And yet, you still married me?"

His expression eased, "Yes, I love you."

She had a tear ease down her cheek as she looked down, "And his estate?"

Byron swallowed a lump, "All yours to do whatever you wish."

She turned a shocked face to him, "What?"

He eased closer and pulled her to his lap, "That is yours. I did not marry you for money. I have plenty of my own."

She cupped his face and kissed him. Byron pushed the kiss further as his hand slid under her dress and up to her thigh. She leaned her head back and moaned as his thumb stroked her core. He was lost in her sweet face and sighs until he couldn't take it anymore. She squeaked as he pulled her from his lap and laid her on the soft quilt. He hovered over her as he kissed her soft lips while easing up her dress.

Her little hand stopped him, "Wait! Not here!?"

Byron smiled as we whispered in her ear, "No one is around, I promise."

She slightly pouted her lips as he placed quick firm kisses on them and continued with his seduction. Caroline gasped as he eased into her and slowly thrusted. She smiled as she felt a warm summer breeze touch the top of her bare thighs. Byron pushed up over her so he could see her face, "Your perfect." He bucked deeper as she moaned loader. Caroline didn't realize, but she had slightly dug her nails into his wrist as her climax grew closer.

Byron thrusted harder and quick until he lost control from her orgasim. He deeply sighed as he came as pressed his lips to hers.

On the carriage ride back to the house, she leaned her head on his shoulder, "Byron?"

"Yes Caroline?"

"I'm very sorry about your mother. I'm sure she was lovely."

Byron affectionately wrapped his arm around her shoulder and kissed her forehead, "Thank you." He glanced down at his sweet wife as his heart broke for her quietly, "I'm sorry for what happened to you. You were innocent."

Caroline sighed as her eyes eased closed and she fell asleep on the way home.

*************Did you like this chapter?

What was Caroline's dream about?

Chapter 21

Byron sighed as he watched Caroline walk onto the main porch. He turned to his younger sister, "Abigail.."

She fluttered her eyelashes to her brother, "Why yes Byron?"

He then turned his love sick eyes back to Caroline as she approached the carriage, "Why must you dress her so..."

"Seductive? Beautiful? Voluptuous?!"

Caroline paused her walking as she heard Abigail. Byron growled at his sibling, "Yes, all of those?"

Abigail chuckled and patted his arm, "She's my little doll. I didn't have one for so long, I'm catching up for lost time."

Byron grasped Carolines dainty hand and helped her in the carriage. She cocked a questionable brow, "What were you two discussing?"

Byron growled, "Nothing.."

He eased his temper when he noticed Carolines sad expression as she looked down, "Forgive my tone, Abigail was just explaining why she dresses you.." He stopped as she looked to him with large sad eager eyes, "So.."

Abigail rolled her eyes, "What he means to say, is that he does not approve on how I dress you, but his reasons are completely impossible."

Byron scoffed to Abigail, "Impossible?! What do you mean?"

"Brother, you could dress her in rags and she would still be the talk of Charlestown. So why not dress her in style and make all other women jealous?"

He smirked to her, "Except you?"

"Of course, she is my creation. Why would I be?"

Byron chuckled to his sister but it soon eased as he noticed Caroline fanning herself and looking away with a sad expression. Abigail noticed what caught his attention and kept quiet for the remaining ride to the Drayton's social barbecue.

Byron held Caroline back as she exited the carriage, "Why were you so upset?"

Caroline looked away as she continued to fan herself, "I.."

He pulled her closer, "Go on.."

She sighed as she wrinkled her brow on the verge of tears, "Its difficult enough to be blind, but you nor your sister took in consideration of my presence while conversing on my clothing as though I wasn't present." Byron was shocked and continued to listen, "I know it may seem silly to you, but.. I wish everyday that I might be able to see for your face for only a moment. When you joke about my appearance that I have no control over, well.." Her lip quivered as she looked down to hide her tears, "It hurts.. deeply."

Byron placed his palm on her cheek and stroked a tear away with his thumb, "I am so sorry Caroline, please forgive me."

She placed her hand on top of his and turned her face to place a kiss in his open palm. He gently tucked her arm into his and slowly ushered her to the social. As Byron conversed with other gentlemen, he watched Caroline and Abigail from a distance. Caroline sat silently and nervous from the other females chattering. Abigail gently patted her leg and whispered in her ear, "I'll be only a moment."

Caroline shyly nodded and smiled as Abigail took her leave to go to the Lavatory. Byron squinted his eyes at an approaching Sylvia. As he was about to intercept, a smug Ashton Henson blocked his path, "Congratulations on your bride. She's lovely."Byron balled up his fist ready to strike. Ashton noticed his actions and stepped back, "Easy now. I was wondering, do you think she would be able to tell a difference if another man had her?" Byron slowly turned a frightening, calm , cold blooded killer look to him. Ashton smirked to his expression, "Just curious."

Byron slowly tilted his head as it popped loudly, "Touch her and it will be the end of you." Ashton held up his brandy glass in a cheers motion and watched as Byron walked to save Caroline from Sylvia.

As Caroline anxiously awaited for Abigail's return, she heard Sylvia's familiar voice, "Hello ladies. What is the subject of your conversation?"

Hanna Clark, a young woman that was just engaged giggled, "Marriage and children! Oh Sylvia! How many children would you like to have?"

Sylvia smirked, "None.."

All the other ladies gasped and scoffed. All but Caroline. Sylvia cut her eyes to the young beauty that had stolen Byron's heart, "What say you Caroline? Oh but wait.. I suppose Byron will be giving up his dreams of children since he settled for you."

The other ladies gasped again, but none came to her rescue. Caroline gathered her courage, "Why would he be giving up children? I don't understand?"

Sylvia cackled, "Did you hear her? My dear, you're useless. You are only a poor excuse of decoration. How can you take care of a baby when you can't even take care of yourself? Really? Blind and simple minded.."

Caroline couldn't believe the cruelty that Sylvia's tongue could produce. Sylvia smirk turned into a smile as she noticed Byron approaching. She could tell by his expression, he knew what she had done, "Hello Byron darling. I was telling your simple, plain wife that children are clearly out of the question. Maybe you should explain to her how silly her idea of having children is."

Byron glared at the evil witch, "If only..I could hang you from the closest tree.. Even though nobody else would admit it, I promise you they would enjoy it."

Sylvia's smile disappeared as she glared at him. He always had a few words to stab her heart. This infuriated her, "Congratulations on your marriage, I'm sure she will make an excellent ball and chain."

Byron steeped closer and whispered a chuckle, "Did you know how your dear fiancé received his black eye?"Sylvia's eye twitched as Byron continued his taunting, "He tried to seduce my amazing, exquisite, and I dare say, well formed wife. If you disagree with me, you need your eyes examined."

Sylvia's lips twitched as she growled. Byron stepped back and eased Caroline from her seat. He turned a cold glare to the other females, "Ladies, you should be highly disappointed in yourselves. I hope one day the same protection that you bestowed upon my wife falls on you. Good bye." He slightly nodded and escorted Caroline away from their shocked faces.

******************Did you like the chapter?

Did Caroline have a right to feel upset?

Chapter 22

Caroline sighed as she soaked in the large medal tub. Her thoughts were thrown back to what Sylvia had said, "Completely useless." She snapped out of her trance as she heard Byron enter the room. He quietly eased down next to the tub and studied Caroline as she tried to cover herself. Her voice quivered as his hand slid up her leg, "Byron please."

"What is wrong?" His hand continued to slide up.

She gasped as his thumb stroked her inner upper thigh, "We need to talk."

Byron sighed as he scooped her from the tub, "Okay."

Caroline jumped as he pulled her from the warm water, "What?!"

He gently placed her feet on the floor and proceeded to dry her off, "What did you want to talk about?"

She felt nervous and vulnerable standing naked before him, "About what Sylvia said."

He paused his drying and stood straight, towering over her, "Caroline, you would be an excellent mother, sight or no sight. Do not let her put doubts in your perfect little head."

"How will I take care of it? When it learned to walk, what if it gets lost?"

Byron pulled her to him, "Caroline, I will be here. Abigail and Gregory will be here. I will get the best Mammy (Southern slave word for Nanny) I could find. I want children with you. If it is Gods will."

Caroline wrinkled her brow as she was still thinking about what he said. He leaned down and placed a sloppy kiss on her cheek. She slowly started to accept them. Byron had lust filled eyes as he lifted her and placed her on the edge of their bed. He towered over her as he pressed his warm wet lips to her soft neck. Caroline whimpered from the intense pressure of his kisses. He lost all restraint from her little noises and stripped off his clothes. She pressed her eyes as he slipped into her and bucked hard and quickly. Caroline threw back her head as she leaned back on her hands. Byron stared at her face as he pounded, "I love you. I want you with child." Caroline gasped louder as his words sent her over the edge and spasmed around him. He continued his rough pounding. He never made love with such force, but he couldn't think of a better way of showing her how bad he wanted her pregnant.

Caroline felt unbelievable pressure building between her legs for a second time. Byron smirked at her squirming as she couldn't bear all of the sensations. She then cried out, "Byron please!"

He grunted as he thrusted deeper while reaching down and flicked her clit. Caroline cried out in what sounded like agony, but it was her release. Byron threw his head back and spasmed inside her.

Caroline laid in bed with her back pressed against a snoozing Byron. She smiled as her hand reached up behind her and caressed his cheek. Byron's eyes slowly fluttered open. He turned his mouth and kissed the inside of her palm. When she shifted against him, she could feel his excitement as it pressed against her bare backside. Byron nudged her legs apart and slid in from behind and slowly thrusted. She smirked and sighed as he pressed her closer to thrust deeper. He groaned as he squeezed one of her firm bouncing breast as he bucked. Caroline was squirming as her climax approached. Byron's breath hitched every time he quickly thrusted. He sent goosebumps all over her as he whispered in her ear, "I'm so close.. Mmm... Cum for me.." he removed his hand from her breast and gently stroked her clit. Caroline cried out as she finally shuddered from her release. Byron growled as he pressed his loins closer as he came.

He was about to shift away, but Caroline stopped him, "No, stay. I want you inside."

He lightly kissed her temple and hugged her close. Caroline sighed with a smile as her eyes drifted close for the night.***************

Chapter 23

Byron eagerly banged on the library door, "What are you two doing in there?"

Abigail snickered, "I'm stealing your wife's affection.."

Byron's eyebrows shot up as he flung open the library door. Carolines mouth was open in shock as Abigail chuckled while sitting across from her, "Oh, hello brother."

He growled as he walked in, "Abigail, please try to keep your perverted mind from my innocent wife."

"Sorry brother."

Caroline blushed as she looked down when he approached her, "Abigail.."

She rolled her eyes, "I know.. You want to see your innocent wife in a not so innocent position."

He cut a cold glare to her as she retreated from the library. Caroline sighed a nervous sigh as she heard him lock the door. Her heart raced as she felt him sit next to her. He didn't say a word, but gently kissed her until she pulled away, "Byron..?"

"Hmm..?" He moaned against her cleavage.

She tried to keep her breathing in check as he deepened his kiss on her bosom, "I.. well.. This is the third time today.."

He leaned away to study her scarred face, "Keeping count?" He leaned back in to continue his seduction.

She gasped loudly as he pulled her from the couch. He spun her around as he feverishly stripped the ribbon from the back of her dress while placing kisses on her bare shoulders. Caroline whimpered as he cupped her front sensitive bud and stroked. Byron moaned as he pressed his flesh to hers and roughly pulled her to him. She was slightly caught off guard with his roughness, "Byron..?"

He smirked as he realized his actions were freighting her, "I'm sorry. I just can't get inside you fast enough."

Byron sat his naked body down on the sofa and pulled her back safely on his lap. Caroline sighed little noises as he reached around and grabbed a firmbreast. She gasped as he spread her legs and thrusted inside her while he held her as he thrusted. Her brow wrinkled as she leaned her head down from the overwhelming sensation. Byron threw his head back against the sofa as he guided her hips. His grip became tighter as he thrusted faster.

Caroline whimpered loudly as she leaned back against his hard chest, "I'm cuming.."

Byron pressed his teeth as he grunted with his last thrust, "Aaahhh.."

As they laid on the couch Caroline smiled, "I hate to break it to you, but Abigail and I will be going into town tomorrow. I don't think they allow such public affection."

He chuckled against her neck, "I will go with you tomorrow, and will try to control myself."

"Byron."

"Hmmm?"

"I love you."

He smirked and pulled her closer, "I love you too."

The next morning, the trio sat out for town. Byron was still clueless for the purpose of the trip, but kept his curiosity to himself. When the carriage stopped in front of the doctors establishment, Byron couldn't contain himself, "Are either of you ill?"

Abigail giggled, "Only in my mind brother. Come Caroline."

Byron did a double take to both ladies, "What is this about?"

His sister smiled, "Personal matters Byron."

He pursed his lips as he watched them enter the office.

Caroline sat on the examination table as he covered one eye and studied the results when he uncovered it. He smiled at the outcome, "When did your eyes start to improve?"

"Three days ago. I cannot see far away but it is getting better day by day. The only issue is headaches, about mid day."

The doctor scratched his head, "I would suggest just taking a rest when they come. Go to a dark room and lie down. A cold compression might relieve the tension also."

Abigail and Caroline both thanked him and headed to the carriage. Abigail and Caroline both froze as they spotted Byron being released from a kiss by another woman. Caroline quickly grabbed Abigail and whispered, "Do not tell him of my sight. Do you understand me?"

Abigail quickly cut her eyes to her brother, "Of course."

Byron snapped his head to his furious sister and a hurt Caroline. "Dear God! Did they see him? He was innocent! The woman was a first time fling, nothing more. She kissed him." He nervously cleared his throat, "Rebecca, meet my sister Abigail and my wife Caroline."

Rebecca snapped her head to him, "Wife?"

Caroline tried to keep her gaze as normal, but with her sight returning it made it difficult. Byron stepped to her and lightly tried to usher her with his hand, but she pulled away, "I.. I can manage.."

Byron frowned at her reaction as he tried to figure out how she knew. Surely Abigail did not tell her since they both were shocked. He looked to Caroline, "Is everything alright?"

She continued to keep her face turned away, "Yes why?"

He gently tried to hold her hand but, she gently moved it out of his grasp. He slightly growled, "Are you sure?"

Caroline had tears come to her eyes, "Of course."

****************What will happen next?

Will Byron go back to Rebecca?

Will Caroline stay?

What if she is pregnant?

Chapter 24

When the carriage arrived, Byron made it a point to touch Caroline as she exited the carriage. She shivered as he slightly squeezed her arm and pulled her to him, "Here, let me help you."

Caroline squeezed her eyes as she felt his breath on her cheek. She turned away as he tried to kiss her. Byron stared at her with an angry glare, "What is it?"

His expression eased as tears spilled on to her cheeks, "I don't feel well. I'm going to lye down."

He slowly released her arm and watched her head into the house. Abigail watched her with sad eyes as she passed by her. Byron locked his eyes on his sister and walked to her, "Im not unfaithful to my wife."

Abigail sighed, "I didn't tell her what I saw, but that doesn't mean she couldn't feel her heart breaking."

Byron swallowed a lump in his throat as he walked away.

He hesitated before opening the bedroom door, but slightly gasped as he opened it. Caroline was slowly trying to unhook the front of her corset but was having difficulty with her eyes focusing. She gasped when the floor creaked as he entered, "Its just me."

Her mouth went dry as he kneeled down in front of her and moved her hands. Carolines chest heaved as he undid the difficult garment.

Her eyes widened as he scooped her up and carried her to the bed. When he tried to kiss her again, she turned away, "Im sorry, but I do not feel well. I just want to lye down please."

Byron never had forced himself on anyone, but her reluctance was driving him mad, "Very well. May I lay with you?"

Her lip quivered as she nodded. Byron himself was on the verge of tears, "Im sorry for what ever I did to you."

Caroline swallowed a sob and nodded. He kissed her brow and tucked her in. Her eyes finally closed and she drifted off to sleep.

Byron felt terrible about kissing his first infatuation, but she came on to him. His guilt started to mock him, "What would you had done if you found her in the same situation?"

He growled as he answered himself, "I would kill the bastard and lock her away so it would never happen again." Of course he knew that would be ridiculous, but he couldn't stand the thought of another man touching her, and her accepting it. He would confess what he did an face the consequences, she deserved the truth. Byron sighed at his uneasiness and drifted off to sleep with Caroline curled up next to him.

When Caroline awoke, Byron was gone. She dressed and headed down to the lower level to find him. As she approached the back veranda, she heard his voice mixed Rebecca's.

She peeked out as she noticed Rebecca crying, "You said you would always care for me! What has changed?"

Byron leaned his head back as he sighed, "I am a married man!"

Rebecca slowly eased to him and stroked his cheek, "She would never know. With her blindness, we can be together again." She leaned in and kissed him again.

Byron leaned back quickly as their lips touched, "Im sorry, but no."

Both of their heads snapped to Caroline as she walked out on the porch, "Byron?"

He gulped as he was now caught twice in the same damn day, "I'm here dearest."

"Who are you speaking with?"

Rebecca glared at the younger beauty, "Hello Caroline, we met in town."

Caroline sighed, "Hello again."

Byron turned a cold face to Rebecca, "She was just leaving."

Rebecca quickly snapped an angry brow to him, "Yes, goodbye Byron."

Caroline held her breath as Rebecca strolled past her and rolled her eyes.

Byron slowly stepped to Caroline and held out his hands to her, but he stopped when she stepped away and looked him square in the eye, "I see you Byron. I see what you really are."

He was on the verge of tears, "How long have you had your sight back?"

Her lip quivered, "Long enough."

He shook his head as he tried to touch her but she stepped back again, "This was a ... I want to free you. I want a divorce."

He could feel his blood pressure rising as he proceeded the words, "No!"

She flinched at his anger and closed her eyes, "Please, do not make this more difficult than it already is. I will go back to England, and we won't see each other again."

"What if you are carrying my child? What then?"

Carolines anger finally appeared, "I will raise it myself or remarry!"

His anger boiled over, "Who would marry an uneducated woman?" He couldn't believe that he spoke such evil.

Caroline barely whispered, "You did." and quietly left.

************What will happen next?

How can Caroline find it in her heart to forgive him?

Chapter 25

C aroline sat on the large porch as she rocked with pressed eyes. It was early morning and she was fighting nausea. She stopped her motions as she heard Byron stepped out to join her. He gently touched her brow for her temperature, "You feel feverish, are you feeling well?"

She rolled her beautiful eyes as she tilted her head away, "Yes."

He sighed his irritation away, "Are you ever going to forgive me?" He kneeled down in front of her and grasped her hands.

She looked past him in a daze, "Why does it matter what an uneducated woman thinks?" She then cut her eyes to his.

Byron growled as he pushed away. Caroline yelped and jumped as he threw the rocking chair that was next to her smashing it in the process.

Abigail came out to see the commotion, "What happened?"

Byron rubbed his mouth as he calmed down. He heaved as he turned to a silently crying Caroline. He didn't look away as he spoke, "Leave us Abigail." She silently nodded and took her leave. Caroline whimpered as he leaned over her as he placed both hands on both sides of her chair, "Why do you hate me so?"

"I.. You hurt me. I know you had women before me, but you promised me there would be no other after me. Yet, I catch you kissing the same woman in the same day. It would be best if we end this now. "

Byron had tears ease into his eyes, "Do not do this. I do not want Rebecca. I only want you. Please believe me."

Caroline leaned and caressed his face, "Byron I still love you, but I do not trust you."

His eyes widened as he grabbed her hand, "I have not been with anyone else. I don't want anyone else. I will not release you from me. If you leave, I will find you."

She wrinkled her brow with worry, "I don't understand. I am giving you a way out.."

He pushed away to hold his temper. He heaved as he chose his words carefully, "I breathe to love you, to hold you, to kiss you, to spend rest of my life with you. If you leave, I have no reason to live. You will make me a desperate man. I don't want to go on without you." Caroline pressed the back of her hand to her mouth to hold in her cries while placing the other on her abdomen. She thought about the baby she carried and it being fatherless. Sure, she had threatened to remarry, but she couldn't stand the thought of another man touching her. She calmed her breathing as he continued, "Even though you saw Rebecca coming on to me, you have no idea of how happy I am that you can see again. Even if it means losing you."

Caroline couldn't take it anymore. She eased from her seat and gently grasped his hand and squeezed it, "Byron?"

He turned to her with a tear soaked handsome face, "I will try, but so help me, if I catch you with some other woman.."

He didn't let her finish before pulling her into a hug, "Thank you. I love you dearly. Please know that."

She sighed and nuzzled into his jacket, "I love you too." Carolines brow wrinkled as she kept the thought of her pregnancy a secret for now. She wanted to be certain that he would be faithful to her before revealing it. If he knew, he would never let her go, even hold her against her will.

He tilted her chin up to him and pressed a kiss on her fevered brow. Byron had concern written all over his face for her health. She looked pale and exhausted from the lack of sleep from their disagreement. He wanted to kiss her badly, but wanted to respect her space. Having her around within his grasp had been torture since she rejected his affection, maybe she knew that and was trying to spare him, "Caroline?"

"Hmm?"

" Are you sure you are feeling well?"

She looked away as he studied her features, "Yes, I'm just tired is all." Her eyes eased up to his, "You look tired, husband."

He smirked at her words, "Well please come rest with me wife. These two weeks without in my bed have been Hell."

She shyly looked down as she bit her lip, "Just to rest?"

Byron stroked her cheek then the bottom of her lip, "Of course."

Byron bit his lip as Caroline eased out from behind the dressing screen. She tipped toed to the massive bed and eased in beside him. He let out a deep sigh as her wrapped his arm around her waist. He smiled as he inhaled the familiar scent of her hair, "Sleep well."

Caroline had already dosed off in his arms. Between the empty bed and pregnancy, it had taken its toll on her strength. Byron propped his head on his elbow as he watched her sleep. He smiled as he leaned down and placed a soft kiss on her lips without disturbing her.

**************Did you like the chapter?

Do you believe Byron is sorry?

Is it right for Caroline to keep the pregnancy a secret?

Chapter 26

B yron smirked as he held his eyes closed, "What are you doing Caroline?"

Caroline couldn't contain her chuckle, "No peaking." He sighed as he waited for his surprise. "You may open your eyes now." She smiled a shy smile as she stood before him. Byron's smile eased as he studied the framed drawing in her hands. It was a portrait of Abigail. Caroline had captured the young mother to be perfectly. Byron eased from his seat and took it from her to study it closer. Caroline was beginning to worry if he didn't like it, since he hadn't spoken. She nervously fumbled with her fingers, "Do... Do you.."

He quickly cut her off as his on the verge of tears face snapped to hers, "It's wonderful. Thank you."

Caroline looked down as she spoke, "I didn't know what to get you for your birthday, but I noticed she had a portrait in her wedding gown, I figured she would like to have one like this, then maybe one after the baby's born."

Byron gently sat the gift on his desk and pulled her closer, "Thank you. I couldn't ask for a more sincere gift."

He leaned in and lightly kissed her on the corner of her mouth. She closed her eyes as her finger tips lightly touched the side of his face. Byron hovered his lips over hers, daring for her to kiss him. Caroline pressed her eyes as she pulled away, "I'm sorry.. I.."

Byron sighed as he cupped the side of her face, "It's alright. I love you."

She looked up to him as a tear traced down her cheek, "I need to rest, my headache has returned."

Byron smiled and kissed her hand as he took it. She sighed as he tucked her arm into his and lead her to the bedroom. He laid quietly as Caroline appeared from the dressing screen, "Byron, I can't seem to manage this last hook."

He chuckled as he walked to her, "My pleasure." His smile widened as she shivered when he placed a kiss on her bare shoulder, "Cold?"

She nervously shook her head, "Mmm..? No.."

He hesitated for a moment but then placed another kiss close to the last one. Her breath quivered after he placed another one on her soft skin.C arolines chest heaved while she wrinkled her brow, she wanted to give in, but something was holding her back. Byron's lips pursed as she stepped away, "Are you alright?"

Caroline nervously shook her head as she looked down, "I don't know.."

He stepped in front of her and stroked her cheeks, "Why are you upset?"

Her lip quivered as she rubbed one of his wrist, "I do want to be with you, but.."

Before she knew it, Byron pulled her to a strong kiss. Caroline eagerly kissed him back as she pushed the doubt from her mind. She whimpered as he pulled her chemise from her shoulders and let it fall to the floor.

Byron broke their kiss long enough to scoop her up and carried her to the bed. Caroline watched as he quickly undressed and eased on top of her. Byron paused for a moment, "If we need to stop, you have to tell me now." Caroline looked away with worry. Byron licked his lips as he nuzzled her neck. She swallowed a delightful sigh as he kissed her neck. Byron smirked as she gasped when he grabbed a firm swollen breast.

Meanwhile down stairs, Abigail watched as Oliver opened the door to Miss Rebecca, "Hello Abigail. Is your brother home?"

Abigail smirked an evil smirk, "Why yes, but I believe he is alone laying down with a headache."

Rebecca smirked back as she strolled past her. Abigail turned to Oliver as he shook his head with disapproval. She rolled her eyes, "Come now! You're going to watch her burn too. Let's go before we miss it."

Oliver eagerly followed Abigail up the stairs.

Byron was leaning over Caroline as he bucked deep and hard in between her raised legs, "Oh God!"

Caroline panted as she spoke, "Don't stop!"

Byron pressed his teeth as he continued to thrust. Caroline screamed out with her orgasim. Byron moaned as he spasmed.

It was perfect timing as a shocked Rebecca opened the bedroom door and gasped, "What is this?!"

Caroline quickly covered herself as Byron pulled her up to him, "What the Hell are you doing in our room?"

Rebecca shook with anger as Abigail strolled in, "Oh, I'm sorry brother. Thought you were alone."

Rebecca growled loudly as she stomped from the room.

Abigail chuckled and winked as she closed the door behind her.

Byron looked down to a worried Caroline, "I'm sorry that happened."

She cocked an eyebrow and smirked, "I'm not."

He chuckled a seductive laugh and eased back on top of her for round two.

************Did you like the chapter?

Did Caroline forgive too soon?

What will happen next?

Chapter 27

Byron nipped at his fingertip as he studied Caroline while she drew. She was so into her drawing, she jumped at a knock at the parlor door. Byron sighed, "Enter."

Oliver cleared his throat, "Miss Caroline, there is a Mr. Harry Kingston here to see you."

Caroline's eyes perked up and quickly placed her note pad down as she headed for the door, "Thank you Oliver.."

She gasped as Byron bolted and blocked her path, "Who is he and why is he here?"

Caroline stepped back. She had seen him angry, but this was different, this was pure anger and dangerous jealousy. She rounded up her courage, "Byron, please let me pass.."

He slowly but tightly grasped her arm, "Tell me.."

She searched his eyes, "What has gotten into you?" She wench when he squeezed tighter, "Byron..? You're hurting me.."

He snapped out of his darkness and quickly stepped away. He couldn't look at her after what he did, "Forgive me."

She slowly stepped to him and stroked his cheek, "Come with me." He turned his worried expression to her as she took his hand and lead him to the front porch.

Harry slightly bowed and smiled at the couple as the walked to greet him, "Caroline is it?"

She nervously smiled, "Yes, and this is my husband Byron."

Byron cut him a cold glare as he shook his hand. Caroline had tea served on the back veranda as they talked. Harry showed excitement as he discussed his visit, "I was thrilled when Abigail wrote to me. I think a guide book for the blind would be a splendid idea. What made you come up with this venture?"

Caroline fumbled with her fingers, Byron took one hand into his and squeezed her to go on. Caroline pressed her eyes, "I had an accident almost four months ago. I temporarily lost my sight. I... I never felt so alone, but Abigail saved me. She never gave up. She helped me learn the house inch by inch, how to distinguish people's footsteps... I could go on and on. I just want to help others."

"Why would you not write the manuscript yourself?"

Caroline sighed as she looked to him, "I cannot read sir."

Harry now felt guilt for asking, "I see.."He watched as Caroline looked down in shame. "I would be honored to write your book. I would need Abigail's help of course."

Caroline smiled as she looked to him, "I think she would like that."

"Then it is settled! We will start next quarter. My wife is due any day, and I promised nothing would keep me detained."

Caroline eased off of the couch and shook his hand, "That's wonderful, next quarter then."

Harry turned and smiled to Byron as they shook hands, "You must be very proud, she is a very brave woman."

Byron turned a sad expression to Caroline, "I am, I truly don't deserve her."

Carolines eyes widened at what he said. They waved goodbye as they stood on the porch. Caroline turned her worried expression to her husband. He had pain in his eyes as she stepped to him. He looked down and shook his head, "I'm sorry for hurting you earlier." She tried to caress his face, but he grasped her wrist to stop her, "I don't deserve you."

Caroline widened her eyes and spoke with a stern voice, "Byron.. Look at me!" He turned his eyes to her as she continued, "If this is your way of asking for a way out.. I tried to give that to you from the beginning. If you are going to leave me now... I will never forgive you.. Never.."

Byron pressed his eyes as he looked away, "I can't forgive myself for hurting you. I .. I didn't realize what I was doing. When you showed excitement from another man's arrival, I went mad. I thought you were giving me a dose of what Rebecca did to you."

Caroline sighed as she paced, "Byron.. I would never wish you any pain. As much as I wanted to.. I couldn't stand to see you feel the same way as I did." She paused as she hung her head, "I love you."Byron stepped to her and pulled her to him. She nuzzled into his chest, "You're suppose to protect my heart, like I'm meant to protect yours, no matter what."

Byron pulled her head up as he cupped her face and kissed her, "I love you Caroline. Please forgive me."

She whimpered as she pulled away from his kiss, "I do, but you have to forgive yourself, or this jealousy will destroy what we have."

Byron rubbed the tip of his nose against hers, "I will try. I promise."

She smiled as she leaned in to kiss him again.

***************What did you think of this chapter?

Will Byron get over his jealousy?

Should Caroline tell him of her pregnancy?

Chapter 28

Caroline smiled as she looked over the goods at the Charlestown city market. Abigail was a few feet ahead of her as she argued with a farmer and his prices. Her attention was turned to someone tugging at her skirt for her attention. Caroline smiled at the small slave child as she kneeled down to her, "Yes?"

The little girl swayed back and forth as sh shyly spoke, "Your sister told me to fetch you. Her carriage is right there."

The little girl turned and pointed to a fancy carriage in the distance. Caroline wrinkled her brow as she studied it, "Was my sister alone?" The little girl shyly nodded. Caroline smiled, "Thank you."

She looked back to a fussing Abigail then back to the carriage. She swallowed her fear and headed towards it. When she almost reached her destination, she stopped, "Lady Elizabeth wouldn't know if I knew about our father." She had the sudden feeling of dread as she turned to retreat.

She gasped as she came face to face with the Duke, "Hello Caroline." He grabbed her arm and pulled a small blade to her abdomen, "If you scream, it will be the end of you and whore of a sister. Understand?"

Caroline nervously nodded. She turned back to the carriage as she spotted the young girl that had tricked her. She was standing next to a smirking Rebecca. Carolines heart broke of the thought of her bedding Byron after they took her. She prayed they would end her misery soon.

****************Abigail sobbed as she paced the front porch, "Where could she be?"

Byron hugged his distressed sister, "I will find her."

Their attention turned to a familiar unwelcome carriage. They both cut their eyes to one another as they released their hug.

Rebecca had a look of sympathy as she approached the siblings, "I must speak with you Byron."

"What ever you have to say, say it in front of us both."

Rebecca flexed her jaw as she stepped up to them, "Caroline has left you. She came to me today before she left."

Abigail cocked her eyebrow, "Why would she tell you?"

Rebecca scoffed, "Because she wants Byron to be happy. She knows his heart belongs to me." Her temper flared when the siblings look to one another in disbelief, "Here is a letter from her. She wrote it before she left." Byron took the letter from her and crumbled it in his hand. Rebecca held back her smile assuming she had won.

Byron gave her a chilling look as she stepped to him, "Get the hell off of my step!"

"Byron?" Rebecca's mouth dropped open as he walked away.

When Rebecca turned to Abigail, she couldn't understand Abigail's smiling expression until she punched her jaw, sending her flying down the steps. Byron and Gregory both ran to the sound of Abigail kicking and pulling Rebecca's hair, "Stupid whore! What makes you think he would ever want you."

Gregory yelled for her to stop as he pulled her off of her, "Abigail! Don't hurt yourself!"

Abigail heaved as she glared at her, "You stupid bitch..."

Rebecca squeaked, "Byron! You believe me..! Right..?"

Abigail chuckled a sick laugh, "She can't read! There is no way she wrote that damn letter!"

Rebecca swallowed loudly as Abigail told what a huge mistake she had made, "Whhaatt..?"

Abigail smirked, "Lock her up. I'm not done with her yet."

Byron roughly grabbed Rebecca by the dress collar and dragged her down into the houses cellar. She pleaded as he chained her to the wall, "Byron! Don't do this! She wasn't good enough for you! I'm saving you."

Byron roared as he back handed her, "Shut your filthy mouth, and pray my sister has mercy on your worthless soul."

Rebecca started to cry after the shock of him hitting her eased, "Byron?! Come back! Byron!"

Gregory met him on the porch after he had locked up her driver and sunk the carriage in the swamp, "What now?"

Byron sighed as he leaned against the porch railing, "Wait for Abigail to get an answer." Gregory pressed his eyes and nodded.

****

Caroline gasped for air as the wool hood was removed from her head. She scanned the ships cabin and was in shock when her eyes fell upon Lady Elizabeth asleep on the bed. She quickly ran to her and squeezed her had, "Elizabeth! It's me.. Caroline.. Wake up!"

Elizabeth moaned and swatted at her, "Go away..."

Caroline shook her head in disbelief. She did a double take as she noticed the empty laudanum bottles on the bedside table. She then turned to the dukes voice, "Sad isn't it?"

"What have you done to her?"

The Duke shrugged and stepped to her, "I can't help it if she likes to self medicate.. She was a empty shell that had to fill her needs by other men. Now it's laudanum." Caroline pressed her teeth as she charged towards him. The Duke growled as he back handed her, sending her to the floor, "But you.. You're definitely a fighter.." Duke Rochester then grabbed and pulled Caroline up by her hair.

She grunted as he slammed her forward against the wall, "Stop! I'm with child!"

The Dukes expression eased as he released her, "Shit.."

Caroline pressed her eyes as she stayed turned away, "What is it that you want?"

The Duke leaned and placed his hands on both sides of her. Her lip quivered as he whispered in her ear, "You.. and your estate."

*************What should Abigail do to Rebecca?

Will Byron find Caroline?

Will her baby survive?

Did you like the chapter?

Chapter 29

Rebecca trembled when Abigail approached her with the red hot poker, "Open up Rebecca.."

Rebecca screamed at the top of her lungs, "Are you mad?! You haven't even interrogated me, and your going to burn my tongue?!"

Abigail rolled her eyes, "Tell me something useful or open your mouth!"She smirked as she eased the poker closer.

"Duke Rochester has her! He abducted her at the market! Said he was taking her back to England, the ship has sailed."

Abigail squinted angrily, "With your help of course?"

Rebecca's chest heaved as her voice shook, "Yes."

Abigail pursed her lips and pressed the hot iron between Rebecca's heaving bosom, "Ooppss.."

Rebecca let out a blood curdling scream, "Why?! I told you everything!"

Abigail giggled as a tear eased down her cheek, "You helped him take someone that was very dear to us. Pray that we get her back."

Rebecca hung her head as she sobbed, while Abigail left the dark cold room.

Both men snapped their heads to the parlor door as it opened, "Duke Rochester is taking her back to England, his ship has already set sail.

Byron sprung from his seat to Abigail, "I know I said I would be here when your child was born.. But.."

Abigail pulled him into a hug, "Bring her home..."

Byron sobbed as he held his sister tight, "I will.. No matter how long it takes."

Abigail and Gregory both waved goodbye as her brother took off to set sail. She had high hopes that her brother would find Caroline safe and sound soon.

****

Caroline held her mouth as the ship swayed back and forth. Duke Rochester curled his lip at her nausea, "I can't believe you already have a bastard in your belly."

Caroline spoke through pressed teeth, "My baby is not a bastard! I was married before God, and my husband is and will be the only man that will touch me."

He rolled his eyes, "Caroline, Byron is probably fucking Rebecca as we speak, the little slut does have some charm."

Carolines cheeks exploded as her nausea took over. The Duke tried to get out of her way, but wasn't quick enough. He cursed as he slung his hands away from his dirty clothes, "You did that on purpose!"

"Well.. You shouldn't talk about such disgusting things.. Even though it's a vast improvement, I wouldn't become ill in your direction."

The Duke glared at her as he took a step closer but stopped when she acted as though she was going to throw up again. He growled as he took his retreat and slammed the door. Caroline smiled at the victory but it soon disappeared at the thought of Byron being with Rebecca. She thought, "Even if I do get away, perhaps it is best to stay away. I couldn't stand to see him with another woman. It would spare my humiliation and his guilt to an uneducated wife. If he really wants me, he will find me." A tear eased down her cheek, "Please want me.."

Byron smirked at Sam's good news, "My informant told me the Duke did not wait for supplies here in Charlestown. He planned on sailing up the North Carolina coast and restock there.

Byron chuckled as he patted Sam's shoulder, "He doesn't stand a chance to out run us. Prepare to sail."

"Aye Captain."

Byron turned to the open sea with a worried brow, "Stay safe Caroline. Please, come back to me."

*************Caroline gasped as the ship lurched from side to side. When she opened her cabin door, she stepped back as a couple of sailors charged to the deck. Her eyes widened as she heard the captain yell, "Abandon ship! We are going down!"

Carolines mind screamed as she ran to Elizabeth's cabin, "Elizabeth wake up!"Elizabeth moaned from her laudanum high. Caroline pressed her eyes, "Please! Wake up!"

She turned a frightened face to the doorway as the Duke charged and grabbed her away, "Time to go!"

"No! No! I won't leave her! No!!"

The Duke growled as he slapped her into submission, "The next one will be to your belly!"

Caroline sobbed as he pulled her from the cabin, "Please! Don't leave her!"

The Duke smirked as the stormy rain fell on her face, "Come Elizabeth, we must get off the ship. Especially for the sake of our unborn child."

Carolines eyes widened in shock. She never dreamed that he would do such a thing. "Byron.. please want me!" , her mind screamed.

As she sat in the small boat, her heart broke as she watched the ship sink along with her sister still on. She promised her, she would seek revenge for her. Duke Rochester was a marked man.

*************Will Byron find Caroline in time?

What did you think of the Dukes plan to switch Caroline with Elizabeth?

How will Caroline escape?

Do you blame her for her doubt in Byron?

Chapter 30

Caroline heaved as she tried to walk onto shore with her soaked dress. She wanted to just lay down on the sand and cry for her dead sister, but Duke Rochester kept a firm grasp on her arm. She looked around the deserted shore for signs of life, but saw none. The captain and crew had gathered wood and built a massive fire on the sandy beach. Caroline sat next to her captor and spoke not a word under his direction. She shivered at the thought of him hurting her and her unborn child. She then thought of Byron and Rebecca, this brought tears to her eyes and a quivering lip. The captain looked to her distressed face, "Don't worry miss. We will be rescued soon, we will keep a fire going and a ship will see it."

Caroline smiled to him, "I lost something when the ship went down."

He gave a sympathetic smile, "I'm sorry ma'am.. Can it be replaced?"

Caroline held back her tears, "Im afraid not."

The captain nodded as he looked down with sadness.

Carolines hopes did raise a little bit with the captains words of them being rescued, she would then have to find a way to get away from Duke William Rochester, but how?

Byron's heart sank as Sam spotted the Victoria's bow floating in the water with the rest of the ship. Byron kept his gaze on the discovery as Sam spoke, "What now Captain?"

"We keep sailing, but change to south east, the current would have carried them that way."

"Aye Captain."

Byron pursed his lips as he turned away from the wreckage.

***************Caroline fought to keep her tired eyes open. William rolled his eyes as she leaned back and forth, "Go to sleep.. No one will harm you.."

She cut her eyes to him and waited for a moment. She eased her expression and nodded. William sighed as he watched his prisoner finally fell asleep. He wasn't planning on harming her, he needed her alive to sign over her fortune. He had hoped to bed her, but with the child in her belly made her seem less appealing in his eyes. He would keep her after she signed since she was easy on the eyes. Williams eyes finally eased closed as he drifted off to sleep.

Byron smiled at the sign of smoke as dawn broke, "Sam! The island! Sail her there!"

"Aye captain!"

Byron's heart pounded against his chest with anticipation. She was so close. He could feel it. She had to be.

Carolines eyes fluttered open as she heard the crew yelling on the shore, "Captain! A ship!"

She leaned up on one arm and smiled at the Saint Furry as it approached shore. Her happiness was short lived as William roughly grabbed her arm and held a knife to her abdomen, "Scream and I'll cut the bastard from your belly."

Caroline looked back to the ship with a quivering lip as the life boats approached shore. Her eyes widened as she noticed Byron on the leading boat. She wanted to yell and scream but she took Williams warning very seriously. She held back a cry as he lifted her to her feet and they made a quiet retreat.

The captains eyes widened with shock after Byron informed him of Williams kidnapping. When he lead Byron to where they were sleeping, his eyes frantically searched the area, "They were just here!"

Byron growled as he turned to his men, "Search every inch of this island!" He turned his angered look back to the captain, "God knows what he will do, to ensure his own escape."

Caroline cried out as William dragged her through the thick jungle of the island. She had severally twisted her ankle that had almost been previously crushed from the dock accident.

"Get up!" William growled through pressed teeth.

She held up her hand to defend herself as she cried when he pulled his knife, "Please! Don't! Give me a moment. I've twisted my ankle. I'm sorry. Please believe me, I would not try to risk the life of my child to lie to you."

Williams expression eased as he saw her true tears, "Get up!"

Caroline hyperventilated as she stood up in pain, "Give me your shoulder.."

William was in shock, but did as she asked. She pressed back a cry as she leaned against him as they walked.

Byron was not far behind, as he was looking at the trail, he stopped as he noticed a folded piece of paper on the ground. His heart felt like it had stopped when he unfolded it to find a drawing of Lady Elizabeth asleep. Caroline had drawn a portrait of her now dead sister before the ship had sank. Byron gently folded it and placed it safely in his coat pocket. He knew she would be pleased to see it again. If she did get to see it again.

*************Did you like the chapter?

How will Caroline escape?

Will William escape?

Chapter 31

William pressed his teeth as he gently eased Caroline down to the cave floor. Her chest heaved as she rubbed her sprained ankle while she caught her breath. William pressed his eyes as he spoke, "I'm going to look for food. Stay here and rest your ankle."

Caroline gave him a worried look, she then turned it to the steep cave side, "What if the tide comes in and I cannot climb out?"

William gave her a cold glare as he stood, "Just stay put, I'll return shortly."

She held back tears as the feeling of dread overwhelmed her. The cave entrance wasn't entirely dark, but with her ankle hurt, she couldn't manage to escape if she wanted to.

***********Byron slashed through the thick vegetation. The humidity was unbearable as him and his crew scoured the island. After hours of searching, Bryon paced as his men took a short rest. His eyes closed with anger as a huge roll of thunder rumbled across the sky, "Bloody Hell!" He turned back to his crew, "Come on lads! On your feet!"

The men quickly stood and followed their captains lead.

**************Caroline breath shook as the cave started to fill with water from the heavy downpour, "No... Oh please no..." Her face wrenched as she stood and back away from the rising water. Her lip quivered as her back hit the caves wall. She looked up to the opening and stared to yell, "Help me! Please!"

William growled as he heard her screams. He dropped the gathered fruit besides the cave entrance and looked down, "Shut.. Up.." His expression quickly turned to shock as he noticed Caroline was shin deep in water, "Oh no.."

"William! Oh thank God! Please come down and help me out!"

William coward back as there was another roll of thunder, "I'm... I'm so sorry Caroline.. I can't.."

Her eyes screamed terror, "What! Get me out of here now!"

William paced at the entrance as the rain poured, "I'm not strong enough to get you out! I can't die.. I'm... to afraid.. I'm sorry.."

He pressed his eyes at Caroline's anger, "Bloody coward! Coward! Coowwaarrrddd!"

William sobbed as he walked away distraught and mumbling, "Please forgive me.."

*************The rain showed no sign of easing. Byron was fearing the worst as the day lingered on. His head quickly snapped to Sam as he yelled, "Captain! Over here!"

Byron ran to Sam, his chest heaved in anger as William sat on the rocky sea shore alone, rocking back and forth, "What have I done?"

Byron roared as he jumped down in front of him, "You bastard! Where is she?!"

William grunted as Byron gave him a mean right hook, "She's dead.. I'm so sorry.."

Byron shook his head in disbelief, "No.. No! Where damn it! Tell me!"

William could barely keep his eyes open, "Cave..."

****

Caroline hyperventilated as she struggled to keep her chin above water. She had tried to kick to stay afloat, but the pain was unbearable. Her eyes widened as as she heard Byron yelling her name, "By..." She gaged and spit the water out of her mouth. She started to cry since she couldn't open her mouth wide enough to scream. Byron's brow wrinkled as he thought he heard a faint cry.

His heart started to beat against his chest as he noticed a rocky edge that eased into the ground, "Caroline!" He turned to the direction of his men and yelled, "Sam! Down here!"

Caroline reached up to him with frightened eyes. Her mouth was now completely covered and her nose was almost submerged. He didn't hesitate another moment as he eased down the cave side slipping and sliding.

He gasped as he slid into the deep cold water, "Caroline! I'm here!"

She took a deep breath as he eased her up out of the water and started to cry, "You found me.. Oh thank God.."

He caressed her face and pulled her into a firm kiss, "I'm sorry I couldn't get to you sooner."

"My ankle, its sprained. Byron, I can't climb out." Her eyes searched his expression as her lip shivered from the cold water.

Byron stroked her face with sympathetic eyes, "I'll get you out." Caroline was in awe of his bravery and calmness.

Sam and the rest of his crew secured a rope and lowered it into the pit. Caroline held on to Byron's back as he slowly climbed up the steep slippery cave side. As they reached the top, Caroline was assisted by Byron's men. She sighed with relief until she spotted a shameful, detained William, "You left me in there to die!"

Sam pulled her off of the prisoner before she could hurt herself. Byron calmly walked over to him and eased him off of the ground and cut his hands lose. Caroline wrinkled her brow in anger, "What are you doing?"

William smirked at him as he rubbed his wrist, "Thank you Byron, now about her estate.."

Byron smirked as he picked William up by the shirt collar and threw him into the flooded pit. Carolines mouth dropped as she leaned over it next to her husband, "I can't believe you did that!"

" Do you want me to fish him out?"

She turned a cocked eyebrow to his handsome face and thought about her dying with her unborn child, "No."

Sam had stayed behind with two crew members to confirm Williams death. Byron gladly carried his injured wife back to the ship to get her warm.

Caroline sighed deeply as he eased her into the brass tub filled with hot water. She closed her eyes and leaned her head against the side until she felt something brush against her foot, then calf. Her tired eyes fluttered open to her anxious handsome husband, "What are you doing?"

"Bathing you..."

Her eyes was back closed again, "I'm so tired.."

Byron tilted his head to the side and studied her, "Are you alright?"

Caroline pouted her lip and nodded, "Yes, just sleepy."

After her bath, Byron eased her from the tub and laid her on a thick towel that was spread out on the bed. He smirked at her figure until he did a double take before wrapping her up. Carolines brow turned to worry as she felt his fingertips lightly touch the little bump of her lower abdomen. She eased her eyes open as she leaned up on her elbows.

She wanted to cry as his face showed amazement of his discovery, "Byron, I'm sorry I didn't tell you.. I.."

He didn't let her finish as he quickly climbed on top of her and kissed her. Caroline cried as she kissed him back, "I'm so sorry.."

He pulled away and shook his head, "Ssshh..." He then went back to kissing her as he removed his clothes.

Caroline was fast asleep, safe and sound in their warm cabin bed. Byron laid away as he stared at the ceiling thanking God that she was there with him.

**************Three years later

Caroline smiled at her son Adam as he studied the chickens in the farm yard of the estate. She loved to hear him speak, "Peep.. Peep.. Hey Moma! Wook! Baby chick chick's"

She leaned down next to him and looked, "I see... I see.. Do you want to go and hold one?"

He gasped with delight, "Uh huh!"

Byron paused for a moment as he spoke with the architect. He bit back a chuckle as he watched his beautiful wife and handsome son play with the farm animals. After his meeting, Byron walked to his little family and smiled, "Good news. He said that west wing was more affordable than we thought. It looks like your school is going to happen."

Caroline smiled as he hugged her and lifted her to a kiss, "That's wonderful!"

The couple both smiled as Adam pulled on his mothers skirt and reached with eager eyes. Byron chuckled as he picked him up and tossed him in the air and caught him.

****

As Byron leaned in the nursery doorway, he felt lust as he watched Caroline tuck the toddler in for his afternoon nap. She shyly looked down as he gently grabbed her hand and lead her to their bedroom.

Byron's mouth dropped open in pleasure as he watched Caroline bounce on his hard member while she rode him. She opened her eyes and smiled as she felt him stroked the little bump that recently appeared from expecting their second child, "Mmm.. I love you Byron.."

He arched his back as he held his orgasim at bay, "I love you too.." His moaning became louder as she rocked her hips faster. Caroline wrinkled her brow as she leaned her head back as she came. Byron's chest heaved as he followed her lead. The couple smiled as they laid in each other's arms, and both wondered if life could get any better.

The end.

www.ingramcontent.com/pod-product-compliance
Lightning Source LLC
Chambersburg PA
CBHW070406200726
48294CB00003B/1107